SEASON

Mark Pearson has worked as a television scriptwriter on a variety of shows for the BBC, ITV and Channel 5, including *Doctors, Holby City* and *The Bill*. He has written four previous Jack Delaney thrillers – *Blood Work, Death Row, Hard Evidence* and *Murder Club* – and was co-author of James Patterson's number 1 bestseller *Private London*. He lives in Norfolk.

Also available by Mark Pearson

Hard Evidence
Blood Work
Death Row
Murder Club

THE
KILLING
SEASON

MARK PEARSON

arrow books

Published by Arrow Books 2014

2 4 6 8 10 9 7 5 3 1

First published in Great Britain in 2014 by
Arrow
Random House, 20 Vauxhall Bridge Road,
London SW1V 2SA

www.randomhouse.co.uk

Addresses for companies within The Random House Group Limited can be found at: www.randomhouse.co.uk/offices.htm

The Random House Group Limited Reg. No. 954009

A CIP catalogue record for this book is available from the British Library

ISBN 9780099574682

Typeset in Sabon LT Std by Palimpsest Book Production Limited, Falkirk, Stirlingshire
Printed and bound by CPI Group (UK) Ltd, Croydon, CR0 4YY

For Lynn,
The love of my life, and for Monti the dog

Prologue

David Webb was a dead man walking – or, rather, stumbling. He was blindfolded, and his wrists were bound tightly behind his back. He could feel the cold, damp wind on his face and he shivered. Dark blood was matting his hair, blood that had left a creeping stain running from the collar on his once-crisp white shirt down to his rumpled trousers that had had military-sharp creases in them just hours before.

'A dead man walking,' he muttered to himself under his breath. He knew that much at least, despite what they had said. Perhaps it was all his own fault, retribution for the flouting of man-made laws in which he himself saw no relevance? But he was the architect of his own misfortune and had not been able to stop himself, much as he had initially fought against his desires. Is it not often said that the way of the transgressor is hard? Had he deserved the happiness he had found in the unlikeliest of places? He hadn't planned to fall in love. These things are out of one's hands, after all – he of all people grasped that reality. But perhaps this was God's punishment for it. Yet the memory of her cornflower-blue eyes, her long dark curly tresses, the way she quirked a smile when he made her laugh, and the sweet musicality of that laugh. He knew he had no defences against that. He knew that if he were to live his life over a thousand times he would always be smitten by her purity and innocence and beauty. He had been charmed by her in every sense of the word.

The men who had struck him and held him while others bound him had lied, of course. They had told him that they were taking him somewhere safe so that he couldn't disclose what he had discovered – they would keep him there till the deed was done, as it were. But he knew each and every one of them. And when he had looked into their eyes he saw neither pity nor regret – just determination.

For his part David Webb wished he hadn't known what he did. But if his death prevented what was being planned he would gladly give his life. Give it in a heartbeat. Even now. Keeping her safe was his all consuming urge. He knew what these men planned to do and the thought of it spiked his heart. It was a forlorn hope but his mind dwelled obsessively on the possibilities of escape. If they left him alone for a while there was a chance. He was a strong man, a very strong man. Not strong enough to prevail against so many, but he hadn't gone down easy. There were a lot of them who would bear the mark of his fist for a long time.

If he couldn't break free he knew exactly what was going to happen, and he couldn't do a thing about it. If he hadn't been gagged so tightly he would have been screaming in fury. But as it was his life was going to be taken and he was powerless to do anything to stop that.

He felt the force of the wind, which had been swirling around him like a tattered cloak, fall away and the sound of it die down gradually behind him as he was pushed forward. The noise in the air was muffled now and the air itself deader. The texture of the ground beneath his feet changed. The harsh crunch of shingle was replaced with softer mud and his feet sank into it. But the winter chill was still bitingly cold and he shivered again as he stumbled and was hauled up roughly. He could smell the salt in the moist atmosphere, could taste it. He had heard that a man's life flashed before him as he neared death. People saved from drowning told such tales. But for David Webb only one thought stayed in his mind. The warmth of his girl's body, the incredible beauty of her smile, the soft arch of her back and the tumble of her soft dark hair. The music in her laugh and the life in her eyes. For her sake he had kept quiet, determined to take his secret to the grave with him. Taking her secret, too. Protecting her in the only way he had left now. Although, given what he knew, maybe it was a futile gesture. A few months' respite, perhaps. But then, he hadn't really been given a choice.

He was brought to a halt, and he put his right hand on a wall slick with moisture to steady himself. He could hear whispered voices behind him, then he sensed someone step in front of him, felt the blindfold being removed from around his head. He blinked his eyes, as much to clear them as to adjust to the dim light. He could just about make out the features of the man who stood in front of him. A childhood best friend. A fellow investor. He could see the steadiness in the man's eyes, the pitiless resolution.

'You left us no choice, David. You do understand that?' the man said.

'There are always choices,' he replied. 'It's having choices that define who we are. As a person. As a nation.'

'I guess you made the wrong choice, then.'

David nodded sadly. 'Just get it over with.'

The man stepped forward and David Webb gasped as he felt cold steel punch in and through his body. He stood straight for a second and then, as his childhood friend pulled the weapon clear of his body, he sagged to his knees. David looked up at his executioner and a smile played on his lips even as a small trickle of blood dribbled over them. 'You haven't won,' he said. Then he collapsed to the floor. The other man watched him for a moment or two, some emotion flickering in his eyes, but it wasn't pity or regret. He nodded to the men who stood behind the fallen body of the schoolteacher.

'Let's finish this,' he said.

David Webb convulsed where he lay, gasping out her name with his last breath. A prayer.

A sea fret crept in and slowly shrouded the coast from Overstrand to Blakeney. It climbed over the cliffs of Sheringham, draping the golf course that lay eighty feet above the beach in a wet shroud of white mist and creeping up into the pine forest that stretched out on the top of the rise a hundred feet or so above. The cold, if not the fog, crept in through the open doorway of All Saints Church in the parish of Beeston Regis. It was a medieval church with a stone floor and walls. But it wasn't the chill that made Ruth Bryson shiver as she knelt in front of the altar.

Her long dark curly hair was brushed neatly. Her face was devoid of make-up now, and the tears on her cheek glistened in the freezing air. She made a sign of the cross and whispered a prayer. Then her large blue eyes sprang open as she felt a heavy masculine hand on her shoulder. Her heart hammered in fear as she fought to control her bladder.

She looked up at the darkness that lay behind the stained-glass windows.

What had she done? What in Christ's sacred name had she done? She ran her hand over the necklace he had given her. Though she could not understand the words on the inscription, he had explained them to her and she knew that the meaning of them was stronger and older than language itself.

Ruth stiffened as the grasp on her shoulder tightened and pulled her to her feet, the tears running free down both of her cheeks now.

'It's time,' said a man's voice that was every bit as cold as the touch of the sea fret on her bare shoulder.

Part One

I

Deep in the throat of winter.

Apparently, as I was to discover shortly, we are still technically living in an ice age. The Pleistocene-Holocene to be precise. The one that began about ten thousand years ago. Eight thousand years before Christ's feet walked on lands that, in the big scheme of things, were probably not the green and pleasant hills of England.

What do ice ages do? They stir things up, bring things to the surface. I do pretty much the same thing. My name is Jack Delaney and I am a private investigator. But whereas I uncover things by interfering in the lives of people – people who usually wish that I hadn't – ice ages do the same to land masses. Giant glaciers, as they move, rip up the ground below, millions of tons of ice destroying the earlier landscape in a way that industrialists could only dream of. But whereas those men would build more satanic mills, however sanitised, the glaciers created beauty. Albeit beauty of a different sort. Creating mountains and valleys and glacial lakes. Shaping the wild ruggedness of the North Norfolk coast. A harsh and cruel beauty.

I was drinking some lukewarm filtered coffee and

looking out through a window streaked with rain to the North Sea itself and the stretch of that North Norfolk coastline which lay below the cliff edge some small distance in front of me. If the visibility had been any better I could have looked to the right and seen the spire of Cromer church in the far distance.

The Cromer ridge is where the glaciers from the ice age that we are technically still in stopped, creating a landscape unlike anywhere else in East Anglia. People might tell you that Norfolk is flat. But not on this part of the North Norfolk coast it isn't. The onset of the ice age literally tore it up and over the next few days I was to discover that certain people hereabouts had a mind to do likewise.

Somehow or other, through events partly of my own making, I had ended up here in North Norfolk. A journey every bit as traumatic as that of the 'ice rock' to the hard place that I mentioned earlier.

I was in a large static caravan that I was using as a temporary office. It was based near the cliffs, just outside the town of Sheringham in the grounds of a small farmhouse a quarter of a mile or so away from one of the trailer parks that proliferated on this part of the coast like a rash.

I had been a detective inspector in the Metropolitan Police for many years. Technically I still was. My boss didn't have the good sense to accept my resignation. She had talked me into taking a twelve-month sabbatical and used her not inconsiderable influence – and called in some favours – to make sure that my application was approved. Doctor Kate Walker, my wife-to-be, had co-opted my young daughter Siobhan and together they had talked me into us all coming up here to live for a spell. Away from the madding crowds. As the poet Gray expressed it, 'Along the cool sequestered vale of life' – where people apparently kept the noiseless tenor of their life.

I will concede that in this part of the country, compared to the shrieking heart of the metropolis, the tenor of life, whatever that was, was pretty noiseless. In the main. Just not at that present moment.

Standing in a forty-foot-by-ten-foot tin box with the rain drumming on the roof like a million miniature marching bands, listening to the winds howling and looking out as they battered the foaming waters of the North Sea, I questioned the decision to move here. Not for the first time.

Kate had family ties in the area: she had been born in Sheringham before she moved to London after the untimely death of her parents. I had told her that I wanted out of the Met and she had seized on it. She wanted out of the madness of London full stop, and with our newborn baby girl, Jade, and my eight-year-old daughter Siobhan it seemed like a good plan: Team Walker Delaney escape to the country. I just wished it had been a Caribbean sea that I was looking out at, and not the roiling grey bleakness of this blighted stretch of the British coast. It wasn't as though I was unused to it, mind. I had grown up in Ballydehob, in County Cork on the western shores of Eire. Not far from the 'top of the bottle' as the county capital was called and sitting on the North Atlantic, no less wind-blasted and rain-battered a place than my present locale. Especially at this time of year in the last days of October when the dark nights arrived early, and there was nothing more heart-lifting to a weary soul than the sight of a log fire burning in an open grate in the local. Or *one* of the locals, I should say, as you could practically walk through one door of a pub in the town and straight into the next. Four of them cheek by jowl – as your man with the bald head once remarked – huddled against the ocean that I could hear now, grinding and crashing some hundred feet below me on the shore, and another two pubs further up the road from those four. Not bad for a town on the furthest edges of civilisation.

My thoughts had turned to roaring fires not just because of the miserable weather outside but because it was near lunchtime. Somehow my miserable disposition is heartened enormously by a pint of the black gold in my hand or a jigger of Jameson's swirling seductively in a glass. Hell, enough of those and North Norfolk in the pelting rain looks pretty damn peachy to me. Not that I was allowed to swirl much of the healing fluid any more – not at home, at any rate – by order of the boss. Or should I say bosses, both young and older ones and all of them distinctly of the female gender.

I had almost finished a report for Brian Stenson who owned the caravan park that I mentioned earlier, the one further up the coastline. He wanted some security recommendations. His park had been subject to some ongoing petty vandalism. The sort of thing that usually stopped when 'The Season' ended and the hordes of holidaymakers that descend like a plague of brightly coloured locusts on the town scattered north, west and south. The fact that the caravans were unoccupied made them vulnerable at this time of year. But a greater number of incidents were occurring, and the local plod seemed to be doing nothing about it. I had surveyed Stenson's existing set-up, luckily before Hurricane Norma that was then still ripping towards us had made landfall, and was recommending the usual to him. Sensor lights, taller fences at the points of ingress and egress, some CCTV. No rocket science to it, a patrol now and again by yours truly or someone I could hire more cheaply. Stenson had been pretty clear that he didn't want to spend a fortune, and I had told him to just get a large dog. But he was allergic, apparently.

I took another sip of the lukewarm coffee, sat back at my desk and attached the report along with a list of suppliers I could get discounts from. Another click and the email was sent. One of the benefits of modern science that meant I didn't have to go out in the weather and deliver by hand.

I was closing up the laptop when the door opened. The wind howled in and she walked in with it.

2

'What's the haps, Stretch?' said Laura Gomez as she flipped back the hood of a rain slicker two sizes too big for her. I looked across at her and shook my head, amused.

By rights, given that I had handed in my Met warrant card and hung out my private-eye shingle it should have been a tall husky-voiced blonde or a dangerous redhead squeezed into a dress custom-engineered for purpose, who had walked through my door, asking me to defend her from someone following her. Wasn't quite the case here. Any men following Laura Gomez were likely to be dressed in white coats or blue serge.

'Here's looking at you, kid,' I said, gesturing at her with my coffee cup and taking a last swallow.

'Say what?'

'Don't sweat it,' I said. 'What brings you out here on such a lovely day as this?'

Laura Gomez worked for a local solicitor, Amy Leigh, who put a lot of work my way – like the job for Brian Stenson that I had just finished the report on, for instance.

Laura sat down on the sofa next to the table I was working on and grinned at me. 'Do I need a reason to see you, Stretch?' she said.

'Don't call me that.'

She looked me up and down and smiled. 'Well, tall, dark, blue-eyed and handsome is pretty much a mouthful. The boss said I'd find you here.'

Laura Gomez was a petite Asian woman of twenty. She was five foot nothing of attitude with spiky dark hair and a fashion sense straight out of the Addams family. Her family had come over from Goa, apparently, forty-odd years previously. Her father was an engineer and her mother a beauty queen. Amy Leigh had represented her when she'd been eighteen and up on an assault charge. Her family had disowned her – they considered the way she dressed tantamount to inviting rape and they'd refused to pay for a solicitor. Nice people. Amy was appointed to handle her case. It seemed that a twenty-three-year-old Ipswich supporter with red hair and a failed goatee had attempted to molest her outside the Crown pub on carnival night. He had a gang of mates with him. Laura managed to get away when a group of Norwich City fans took a dislike to the Ipswich shirts the members of the other mob were wearing, but the following day she saw the man who had assaulted her walking out of the kebab shop on the High Street and beat the bejeezus out of him with a left-handed five iron. Which was odd, come to think of it, because as far as I was able to establish she was right-handed and had never played golf. But then, I'm also a security consultant to the Sheringham golf course and I've never played golf either.

Amy had changed Laura's wardrobe, schooled her for the trial and got her off all charges. Amy told me that she had no idea how Laura had ended up working as her PA and had no recollection of offering her the job. But, as she told me, employing Laura was cheaper than buying and feeding a guard dog and, despite appearances to the contrary, the girl was pretty damn good at her job.

'Well, you've found me. What do you need?'

'Anything you've got, Stretch.'

She grinned at me lasciviously and I laughed despite myself. 'What I've got is a wife and two daughters.'

'Why have hamburger when you can have horse meat at home – is that what you're saying?'

'I wouldn't put it quite like that to Kate.'

'No, you're safe, Irish,' she said. 'Just tugging on your lariat.'

There were only a few people I let get away with calling me 'Irish'.

'The boss wants to see you,' she said.

'Now?'

'After lunch is cool. You can buy me a bacon sandwich at the Lobby.'

The Lobby she referred to was The Lobster public house, set back from the coast by about fifty yards and where the roaring log fire I had been contemplating in my mind's eye was to be found.

The walk into town was cold and windy enough for us both to hurry inside The Lobster when we got there. Laura was dressed as if it was summer whilst I had my leather jacket zipped tight. I nodded to the barman as we walked in. He nodded back and held up a Guinness glass.

I grinned at him. 'You'd better get the vampire a Bloody Mary.'

'I'll have a pint of Kronenbourg!' she shouted to the departing barman, who had gone to the back bar where the Guinness was on tap. This was the real-ale bar and I had slowly been brought round to enjoying a pint now and again. Hitherto I had regarded real ale as enthusiastically as I would a glass of pond water. But when in Rome or Paris, like I always say, don't take a taxi. Today I fancied a glass of the Guinness, as they served a decent pint here and, well, you never quite forget your first kiss, do you? Your first love or your first pint of the black magic!

The Lobster was built sometime in the mid-nineteenth century, 1850 or thereabouts. The ceiling had been covered with old maps some time ago, nobody knew exactly when: they were yellowed with age and tobacco stains from back in the happy days when bars really were bars, and you were allowed to smoke, swear, make some noise and generally have a good time without drawing the censure of diners. The walls were festooned with pictures of old lifeboat crews and fishermen, nets hung from the ceiling and there were lobster pots, boathooks, long oars. There were etchings on the old sash windows that looked out onto Gun Street where an old cannon was mounted at the corner of the pub. The blazing fire was large, housed in the original brick-built fireplace and chimney breast, with a brightly polished copper hood above it. It sounds like a dreadful theme pub but it wasn't – it just hadn't been altered for years. Hadn't been got at by the corporate chains and breweries who are seemingly motivated to drive all character out of the public houses of England. That was one thing you could say about North Norfolk – they do pubs well.

After I had drunk a third of my pint of Guinness in one swallow, I looked down the menu and ordered the sausage and mash. It was that kind of day. Laura ordered the *fruits de mer* from the specials board. As it was on my tab, I told her to think again. She ordered a double-stacked burger and a large side order of fries. I looked at her thin frame and shook my head.

'What now?' she asked.

'I reckon you must have hollow bones.'

'Purity of heart, a cheerful disposition and an abstemious nature are the fundamental building blocks of a healthy shape, Jack. Heart, mind and body in perfect harmony.'

'Abstemious! I've seen you at The Crown on a Saturday night, remember.'

She grinned. 'Must be the genes, then.'

'There is something you can do for me.'

Laura rolled her eyes. 'Never trust an Irishman, that's what my grandmother always told me.'

'Did she now?'

'Maybe not. But she should have done.'

'A strictly professional matter.'

She leaned forward, her expression animated. 'So what's the case?' she asked. 'Drug smuggling? Prostitution? People-trafficking, coming in from Holland via the North Norfolk coast and then down to London?'

'There's been a bit of ongoing vandalism up at the campsite along the cliffs. Graffiti, broken fences, locks forced even though the vans are empty.'

Laura gave a disappointed sigh, rolled her eyes again for dramatic effect and shrugged, her blade-like shoulders belying the strength she had in her slender frame. 'The yoot be bored. What are you going to do about it, bro?'

'I want you to find out who's behind it.'

'Why me?'

'Because, like you said, it's probably some feckless youngsters like you with their brains in their toecaps.'

'None taken.'

'And the local flatfeet don't seem to be bothered enough to do much.'

Laura laughed again. 'The police. What use are they?'

I returned her sardonic look.

'Well, you ain't proper police, are you, Jack?'

'Just keep your eyes open.'

'Yes, sir. Eyes peeled, ears to the ground.'

'Well,' I said, looking at her pointedly. 'You're close enough.'

She punched me on the shoulder. 'You kill me, Stretch.'

'Don't tempt me,' I said. 'Come on, let's get you back to work.'

3

Amy Leigh had her offices above a gift shop in Gun Street that ran past The Lobster to Lifeboat Plain, a misshapen kind of square bordered by a café, two pubs and a community hall, with a narrow lane beside it that led down to a slipway and the ocean beyond.

You could pick up a pebble, if you had a mind to, from the lower corner of the Plain and hurl it into the sea. I didn't have an urge to do any such thing just then, so I followed Amy Leigh's young assistant instead, walked into the shop and nodded at the blonde woman in a pink jumper behind the till. She was a friend of Amy's so getting to the office through the shop wasn't a problem for either of them. Wasn't a problem for me, either. The jumper looked good on her.

At the top of the narrow stairs Laura pushed on the nameplate bearing the legend AMY LEIGH & ASSOCIATES mounted on a solid white-painted Victorian door and ushered me in. There was room inside for two large desks and assorted filing cabinets. A thick oriental rug lay on the floor and behind the older of the two desks sat the woman designated by the nameplate. As far as I knew, the only associate she had was Laura Gomez but a woman has to have ambition, I guess. Although Amy's ambitions were not financially driven. She genuinely liked helping people. She looked up and smiled as we walked into her office, paying more attention to the paper bag in Laura Gomez's hand than to me.

'Good girl – you bought coffee and croissants?' she said.

'Girl!' Laura Gomez raised her left eyebrow and tilted her chin.

'Just hand the pastry products over. Jack, take a seat.' She gestured towards a chair opposite her desk. 'I'm sure Laura bought enough for everyone.'

'Out of the ten pounds I gave her she did.'

'Hey, Delaney,' said Laura. 'I'm just a lackey of the capitalist overlords, I don't get paid enough to fund the management. Nor do I wish to be complicit in my own oppression.'

'She's been taking night classes,' Amy explained.

'Dangerous thing, educating the ignorant.'

'Who said that?'

'Margaret Thatcher.'

'You guys crack me up,' said Laura, closing the door behind her as she left.

I took a sip of the coffee. It was good. Better than the poor excuse for it from the filter machine back in my temporary office that I had been drinking earlier. Top of my agenda: buy a proper espresso machine. Get the coffee right and everything else falls into place. Law of detecting number one. Start with the java.

'I'll be with you in a minute,' said Amy and took a large bite of her croissant.

She was single, which surprised me. Maybe the way she ate a croissant put men off. Me . . . I like women with appetites. Probably got me into a lot of trouble in the past. The good thing was that I couldn't remember much of it, which was a bit of a mixed blessing. Maybe it was the wisest move to let Kate and Siobhan drag me out of London after all. I looked at the rain that had started up in earnest again, hammering down onto Lifeboat Plain below us, and smiled a little to myself. At least it was clean rain here.

Amy had nearly finished her croissant so I took another sip of coffee and waited for her to tell me what she wanted.

She was a good-looking woman, five foot five or so in her bare feet, dark honey-blonde hair to her shoulders styled with a casual indifference that she managed to bring off. She was lively, charismatic, had twinkling blue eyes and an intellect sharper than the teeth of those reptiles that Saint Patrick reportedly kicked out of the blessed Isle. She was dressed in jeans, trainers and an 'Old Guys Rule' jumper. I didn't ask. Most of the work she did was legal aid or pro bono-based. Her uncle was a big shot, an old-money lawyer in the city. And the city round here meant Norwich. I'd heard rumours – well, Laura had told me – that Amy's Uncle Warbucks had been trying to recruit her ever since she had left law school with offers of fine offices, a car worth two salaries, money, title, et cetera. The whole heir-apparent-to-the-great-legal-empire thing and she had turned him down on each occasion. She was happier working out on the edge of the known world for people who needed help but couldn't afford it. She was my kind of solicitor.

'Sorry for the casual outfit, Jack,' Amy said. 'Supposed to be a paperwork day.'

I looked down at my own jeans, RM Williams boots that needed a polish, a sweatshirt and a thermal T-shirt under my battered old-and-going-nowhere black leather jacket and flashed her a smile.

'And here's me in my Sunday best. So what can I do for you, doll face?'

'Doll face?'

'I've gone private. Isn't that the way we're supposed to speak?'

'Not in Sheringham.' She laughed. 'Anyway, got another little job for you.'

'What's in it for me?'

'You're drinking it. And there's a croissant in it, too.' She pushed the bag forward.

'You've put my rates up and I paid for them!'

Amy shrugged. 'Inflation – what's a girl going to do?'

'What do you want?'

'I need you to frighten someone.'

'This someone you reference. He or she easily frightened?'

'He. And about as easily frightened as an angry Rottweiler.'

I nodded. 'I guess I'll take that croissant.'

4

At least the rain had stopped.

The sky was a ragged patchwork of crimson-streaked clouds and pale, watery blue sky. I love this time of year when it's cold but bright and the skies stretch miles and miles into the distance, when there's a crunch of frost under your feet and your cheeks glow. Maybe it's the melancholic Irishman in me that makes me prefer late autumn and winter to spring. But I do hate the rain!

I was on the coast road heading west. Out of Sheringham and through Weybourne, progressing around the bump of north Norfolk. The sea was to my right and on the left were the foothills of a ridge that soared several hundred feet or so and was dense with pine trees. Sheringham, as the sign on the shore front promenade proudly proclaims, lies 'Twixt sea and pine'. The coast road is a twisting, narrow old-fashioned one that was not built for the size or the power of modern cars and I had to concentrate. It wasn't my driving I was worried about, or the condition and road-handling capabilities of my old Saab. It was the condition of the brains of some of the other drivers on the roads. It was way out of season now so I couldn't put it down to tourists not familiar with the dangers. But the behaviour of some of them made me think they had some kind of death wish. Seeing as some of them were octogenarians who could barely see over the tops of the steering wheels of their huge 4x4s, it was surprising that they seemed in such a hurry to meet your man upstairs, the fellow with the long white beard and the key to the Pearly Gates. But they certainly drove that way, overtaking on bends and blind hills with the kind of bravura usually seen at Silverstone. This was a long, bleak stretch of road in the dark days of October and luckily there were few other cars on it that day.

The man I had been commissioned to 'frighten' was a builder called Bill Collier who was based in Thornage, a small village just outside Holt, though he covered, seemingly, a pretty wide area. He sounded a particularly nasty piece of work, and none too competent so I guess he had to spread himself further afield to find new custom. I had phoned and arranged to meet him a bit later but first I had set up a meeting with the woman he had, so to speak, diddled. In no way was that a euphemism.

I was just outside Kelling heading towards Cley, by the salt marshes that spread in a rare bit of flatland out to the sea. The sea was darkening again and was flecked with white horses in the near distance as the wind started to pick up. I was keeping my eye on the sky – it didn't look like rain just yet – and suddenly I had to hit the brakes hard and lean on my horn yet again. The old woman who was halfway across my side of the road before she straightened up coming out of the bend didn't even register my presence.

I turned left down a bumpy side road where there was some serious real estate lining both sides. Mostly old, but brick-built and ivy-clad. Definitely never been fishermen's cottages. The Saab bucked and bounced on the rough road and its old shock absorbers creaked and groaned in complaint. I didn't know why the road hadn't been repaired and levelled – the people who lived here could afford a bit of upkeep. I guess they wanted to discourage visitors. No riff-raff welcome. I also reckoned their 4x4s at forty grand apiece, and more, didn't feel the pain as much as my ancient Swedish vehicle did. Kate had been pestering me for weeks to change it, saying it wasn't suitable for country living. She'd traded in her car for a fairly new Golf Estate, which we tended to use when we were out and about 'en famille', as she would say. But I liked my old Saab: we had been through a lot together. And the more Kate insisted, the more I dug my toes in. I had told her, paraphrasing a little from the Bible, that women are born to nag 'just as sparks fly upwards'. She wasn't amused. Maybe my roguish Irish charm was beginning to lose its effect on her. Nah. Never going to happen, I had had to license it as a deadly weapon when I set up in private practice.

I turned left into a drive that ran alongside the immaculately maintained front garden of a small but very pretty clapboard-fronted bungalow that was painted in white with a seaside blue trim. It had been built, by the looks of it, in the 1930s and it made a change from all the pebble-and-flint buildings that were strung along the coast, pretty as they were.

I parked my car behind an old but spotless Morris Minor and rang the doorbell. The door was answered by a sprightly woman who also looked like she'd been built in the 1930s. Helen Middleton. A widow. Five foot six, platinum-white hair, a smart two-piece black suit and facial bone structure that had probably launched a thousand ships back in her day. Her eyes were bright and intelligent and she looked like she weighed about six stone in the pouring rain.

'Mr Delaney,' she said with a completely disarming smile. 'I'm Helen Middleton. No relation. We spoke on the phone.'

I nodded. 'Indeed we did. Call me Jack.' I would have shaken her hand but both of hers were busy. She was holding a small dog who was watching me with alert, suspicious eyes. It looked like some kind of terrier crossed with something else. I'm not great on dog types.

'I'd shake your hand, but I don't want Bruno running out into the road,' she said, as if reading my mind. 'I hope you don't mind dogs?'

'Not at all,' I replied. 'I'm an Irishman.' As if that explained everything. Maybe it did.

'What brand is it?'

'Brand?'

'Sorry, breed.'

'Border Terrier with a bit of Jack Russell in him.

Anyway, come in, come in,' she said. 'We're letting all the heat out.'

I did as I was told and followed her into a small hallway that had framed pictures on the wall and a small occasional table with a vase and flowers in it. I could feel the warmth immediately and unzipped my jacket. Helen Middleton opened a door and we turned left into the lounge of the bungalow.

There was a pleasant smell of wood polish in the air as we entered. It was quite a large room but in immaculate order with not a speck of dust anywhere. Which was remarkable considering the number of small tables and other surfaces in the room. All covered with *objets d'art*. Statuettes, toby jugs, miniature figures. Collectible bottles of brandy that were shaped like books. Boxes. An antique gaming table with some Royal Doulton china on it. A log-burner was blazing cheerily in the middle of the wall to my left. Close to it was a very comfortable-looking leather recliner facing a corner of the room where you might have expected to see a television. But instead of a TV there was a high-end audio set-up. Separates with a CD player, receiver and matching amplifier. To the right and left of them some tall expensive-looking speakers. I could just about make out the strains of some classical music playing – she had obviously turned the volume down on my arrival. On a small sherry table to the left of the armchair was a precariously balanced pile of books. A notepad and pen lay on top of them.

'Mozart?' I enquired.

'Not close and no cigar, I am afraid.' She smiled. 'Mahler's fourth. In G major.'

I nodded. Classical music wasn't really my thing. Unless you counted Johnny Cash, which a lot of purists at the Royal Academy of Music didn't.

'Music is one of my passions, Detective Delaney,' she continued. 'You may note that I do not have a television.'

'I did that, ma'am.'

'Life is to short to waste on . . . what is it they call it? "Moving wallpaper"?'

'I'm not such a big fan myself, truth be told.' I smiled at her. 'And I don't get a lot of time for it nowadays.'

'The strictures of the job?'

'That and a newborn baby, and an eight-year-old daughter and a wife who's a doctor who is also called upon sometimes to work irregular hours.'

'Ah. That would be Doctor Walker, then?'

I raised an eyebrow, always a winner with the ladies. 'Sure now you'd make a pretty fine detective yourself, Mrs Middleton,' I said, sticking in a large dollop of the Ballydehob for good measure.

She smiled tolerantly. 'It's Helen,' she said and put down her dog who immediately started jumping up on my legs, his tail swishing back and forth like a windscreen wiper gone out of control.

I reached down and patted him on the head. 'Hi, Bruno.'

The dog seemed satisfied with that and trotted off happily back to his mistress.

'I certainly don't feel like a "ma'am" and "Mrs Middleton" sounds far too formal.' She held out her hand.

I shook it. It felt like a small, warm bird nestled in mine, but she had a surprisingly firm grip.

'And please call me Jack. I'm not technically a police officer at the moment. I'm on sabbatical.'

'So I understand.'

Helen Middleton leaned down and tickled behind the puppy's ear. His tail became even more manic. Had he been a Great Dane that tail could have caused thousands of pounds of damage to her porcelain collection.

'I have to keep an eye on him. Bruno's always keen to meet people and only has to hear the doorbell chime to go charging across. He's not even a year old yet and he doesn't realise what kind of maniacs drive along the roads around here.'

I flashed her a smile again. 'I've noticed that myself, too.'

'You haven't been here long, Jack?'

'My fiancée was born around here. But no, we only recently moved up.'

'Bit of a change from the big city?'

'It is that, sure enough!'

'Well, you may not have been here long, but Amy speaks very highly of you.'

'That's good to hear.'

'Her people are old family friends.' Helen looked at me appraisingly. 'And I am guessing that Doctor Walker, your wife-to-be, is a very handsome woman.'

I smiled again. 'Why would you think that?'

She winked at me. 'Because you are a very handsome man. If I was fifty years younger I might have given her a run for her money.'

I laughed. 'You'd have barely been at infant school fifty years ago, Helen.'

It was her turn to laugh. 'I can see you've kissed the Blarney Stone, Jack.'

'Kissed it? My family installed it.'

'I wouldn't be surprised.'

I had the impression that she was stalling. Avoiding the matter that had brought me to her house in the first place. Everything in this room seemed so ordered. It was as if she was reluctant to break the sense of security she felt in it.

'The police have been of no use?' I prompted her.

She snorted in response – in a ladylike manner, mind. 'Don't even get me started. No offence.'

'None taken. So you want to show me how bad it is?'

Helen nodded, then led me to the left-hand side of the room and opened the door almost reluctantly. Her eyes glistened as she looked inside. But not with joy. She wiped her eyes with the back of her hand as I looked in.

I could see why she had been reluctant to open the door.

5

William

He didn't know how old he was.

Big for his age, but terrified by the small woman who stood in front of him. She had long, dark curly hair tied back, eyes as blue as eggs in a robin's nest and a hardness in them that was no foil to their beauty. She had a heart-shaped face with high cheekbones, lips like a cut fig. Her skin was pale, almost alabaster, and she wore no make-up. When she smiled and laughed it lit up his world like a Christmas tree. But he couldn't remember the last time she had laughed. Or smiled. She certainly wasn't smiling now.

In her hand she held a long stick, and he already knew that he had done wrong. He looked across the kitchen at the broken fragments of the green-patterned plate he had dropped and he felt his knees tremble. The lady who owned the plate would be annoyed. It was part of a set, a valuable set. And the small woman who held the stick would bear the brunt of that anger. But not in the way that he would bear hers.

Soon after, with his back and buttocks bared, the

stick cut fresh marks over old scars and he bit down hard, determined not to cry or yell.

He couldn't remember the last time he had cried, either.

6

The door from Helen Middleton's lounge opened into the bungalow's kitchen.

Some plastic sheeting had been draped haphazardly, bisecting the kitchen, but the wind blew coldly through, creating a low hum as it set the sheet flapping. Beyond that there was a large hole that had been cut through the kitchen wall and beyond that lay her garden, which looked as well ordered as everything else concerning the bungalow. And past the garden lay the flat salt marshes that led to the coast. And then the North Sea itself, stretching all the way to the North Pole. And the wind, blowing straight from there, blew straight into her kitchen.

I shivered. It was a flensing gale.

'It's an extension, a kind of studio for me. I'm doing a bit of writing and I wanted a view.'

'Nice view.'

'Would be – through a window, if there was one,' Helen sighed sadly.

'What was the deal?'

'They quoted me a price. I had a couple of different firms in. They seemed the most reasonable.'

'Cheapest isn't always the best when it comes to builders.'

'Or women.' She cracked a tiny smile at that. 'An expensive lesson I take it?'

Her ghost of a smile faded. 'And a painful one.'

'What have they said?'

'I have already paid them what they quoted to start with and then five thousand pounds more. Now they tell me they want another few thousand to finish it. I haven't got that to spare. Well, I could, I suppose. But there is a principle involved. I am not getting any younger, Mister Delaney. I may need to draw on my investments for other necessities.'

'Do you have a contract with the builders?'

'Not a formal one, no. Because of the new laws on not needing planning permission for a ground-floor extension if you don't go beyond the property's limits, I didn't get an architect. The pair of them seemed trustworthy. What is it they say about a fool and her money?'

'I don't think you're a fool.'

'The evidence would seem to suggest otherwise.'

'Cynicism is the modern curse. It infects our society like a canker. Trusting people is not a bad thing. You shouldn't blame yourself and we can take care of this.'

'How?'

I smiled wryly at her. 'I have degrees in cynicism, Helen. Distinctions in it. The first thing is to get this room sealed properly so your kitchen is usable. And let me worry about the bad men. It's what I do.'

'Like I say. I do have some small resources left financially.'

I held up my hand. 'Let's not worry about that now. Seems to me these people haven't fulfilled their part of the bargain.'

'The police said they couldn't do anything.'

I smiled again. 'I'm not police, Helen. At least, not at the moment, anyway.'

I pulled out my phone.

'What are you going to do?'

'Guy I know in Sheringham. Retired cabinet maker, puts his hands to most things. I'm going to have him put the windows in and see what needs doing to get the rest finished. We'll have this sorted before you know it.'

'Thank you.'

The relief in her voice was palpable. She bent down to pick up her dog who had come scampering up as he heard the emotion in her voice and was whimpering a little, concerned for her. His tail thumped wildly against her arms and he licked her face as if he had not seen her for a week.

She smiled as the tension leaked from her body. Canine medicine.

I smiled ironically to myself as I finished punching the numbers into my mobile. Dealing with dodgy builders and petty vandals – I felt a long, long way from London.

'Mike,' I said as my call was answered. 'It's Jack Delaney.'

7

It was a couple of hours later.

I had taken my Saab back on the demolition-derby coastal road and managed to survive the journey to Weybourne. I'd also called the builder whom Helen Middleton had had the misfortune to employ and had ascertained, by use of skilful detection techniques, where he was currently working. He was doing some roofing work on a rental property that was located down the coastal road that ran from opposite The Ship public house down to the beach.

I had asked about his availability for a quote and he had said he'd be finished about five and could swing by my house later. I told him I would check with the wife and call him back if that was suitable. I'd asked him how far away he was from a street in Sheringham – where we didn't in fact live – and he gave me the name of the street in which he was working. If I hadn't been a detective maybe I would have made a great telephone salesperson. Then again, I reasoned, I probably didn't have either the temperament or the personality for it.

It was nearly three o'clock when I pulled up alongside

the builder's Mercedes van. I'd guessed that he'd have a van and it would have his name on it, and I'd figured right. You don't get to be made a DI in the greatest police force in the land without that kind of deductive genius. The nearly new Lexus parked next to it, with his sign also on the back window, seemed to indicate that he was doing pretty well out of his building business too. Judging by the way he had ripped off Helen Middleton I wasn't surprised that he could afford a luxury car to go with his Mercedes van.

My carpenter pal Mike Garnet had arrived earlier at Helen Middleton's place with a builder friend of his to weatherproof the kitchen, and to evaluate the damage. By their assessment the job required about three grand or so to finish it off to a good spec. The good news was that there were no major problems with the work that had been completed – barring the fact that Bill Collier's lot had overcharged her by about five grand for materials and hadn't finished the job when they were supposed to. And now they were putting the strong arm on her for more money to do so. Sharp practice. The police seemed to regard it as a civil matter, which is, I guess, where I came in.

Only I wasn't going to be civil about it.

I pulled up in front of the Lexus, got out of the car and walked back to the house.

My experience as one of the Met's finest also led me to deduce that the fact that there were two vehicles parked outside the house meant that there was more than just Collier on the job. I could see one guy on top of a medium-sized ladder, adjusting some guttering that ran just above the mounting for a Sky aerial dish that was pointing south.

He was broad-shouldered man, shorter than me by a couple of inches by the look of him. But heavier. Thick dark hair, a face battered by more than weather in its time. His hands were about twice the size of mine. In his late forties, I would have guessed. Something definitely simian about him. I could see why Amy had said he was not likely to be easily frightened. But a man is worthy of his hire, or should be – and I had a job to do.

'Your name Bill Collier?' I asked.

The man on top of the ladder turned round, looked at me and grunted, growling suspiciously.

'Who the fuck are you?' he replied.

'Name of Delaney, Jack Delaney. And I need to speak to you about a job you did for Helen Middleton.'

'What's it got to do with you?'

'I said I would help her in the matter.'

'How?'

'By my reckoning the job needs a few grands' worth of work to get it finished.'

'And?'

'And you have already overcharged her for materials and supposed labour, et cetera. Ballpark? Five grand, let's say. I want the money from you to pay a competent builder to complete the project,' I said pleasantly. Then I smiled.

It took him a moment or two to take it in. 'Are you out of your fucking mind?'

'Not at all.' I kept the smile on my face.

'Want me to come down there and punch your lights out, then?' He had a Midlands accent – Birmingham or Coventry or thereabouts, I guessed.

I took it as a rhetorical question, but kicked the ladder over just to be on the safe side. Bill Collier shouted in rage as the ladder fell away below him. He flailed, grabbed the Sky dish mounting, and dangled some eight feet from the ground. 'You are a fucking dead man!' he yelled.

'I am just trying to establish a bit of dialogue here. We can do it easy or we can do it hard, Mr Collier. Either way the lady is going to be compensated.'

'Just who the fuck do you think you arc?' His face was red with rage and exertion.

I smiled again and pulled out my warrant card. Somewhat out of my jurisdiction, and, technically, not serving presently. But I figured he wouldn't be able to read the small print.

'I'm all kinds of trouble,' I said and slipped the card back into my pocket. 'You know, and I know, that you have had the woman over. Put it right and we don't have to get official. Everyone's a winner. You don't get sued and she gets her extension.'

'And if I tell you to go stick your head in a pig?'

'Well then, I would have to take action.'

'Don't!' he shouted out suddenly. I was puzzled for a moment until I realised that someone was coming up behind me.

I turned round and saw a man even bigger than the one who was dangling above me.

I reacted on instinct as the newcomer hammered

a fist into my stomach. I moved in time to lessen the impact. Even so, it felt like a steam-hammer. I gasped and staggered back.

'Leave it, Sam,' shouted the man above. But his colleague seemed not to hear him. He swung a slow roundhouse punch to my head. I stepped aside and snapped a fast punch to his jaw. He stumbled, shook his head, looked puzzled and then turned to face me. I shot a quick jab to the bridge of his nose and then a fast left-right combination. He fell to the floor, dazed.

I picked up the ladder and leaned it against the wall, just out of the dangling man's reach.

The other one lurched to his knees, making a ragged, gurgling sound.

'What are you going to do? He didn't know you were a copper,' said Bill Collier, gasping as he struggled not to fall from his precarious perch.

I shrugged. 'Sort out that repayment for Helen Middleton and everything, I am sure now, will be fine. We can put this behind us and just move along.'

'You have no idea who you are dealing with, you fucking mick! You're not going to get away with this!'

'Yeah, I will. One way or another. Up to you how hard you want to make it on yourself.'

I turned and walked slowly back to my car with a confident smile on my face.

I used to play poker, after all.

8

William

His parents had been killed soon after he was born.

He had been told when he had been old enough to realise that he was an orphan. He had never known them and nobody ever talked about them. Not that there was anybody to talk to apart from his aunt. She was his sole surviving relative and she had brought him up without ever sparing the rod. She never mentioned her dead sister or her husband and he learned from an early age that he should not bring the matter up. She seemed to have no friends nor the desire to make any. She worked hard, brutally long hours and he was left pretty much to his own devices. He had no friends, neither in the squalid street where he lived nor in the school he was sent to. He and his aunt had moved around the country before coming to King's Lynn and what little education he'd had hadn't prepared him for much. He wasn't bothered. He was used to being different, other, used to being a loner.

Poverty wasn't an abstract concept in his life. It was a hard-faced reality that ran through every part of their existence like the rings of an oak tree. Their place in the world had been clearly defined for him since he'd been old enough to walk. They were scum. And they deserved no more and no less than they got. Pain, hardship, and sorrow. He had been sent to school finally but that was no refuge. The Brothers were of a cruel and sadistic nature. He had always been a strong boy, but amongst grown men he was as weak as a woman and he knew that. So he kept his head down and minded his own business as best he could. That didn't stop the Brothers using the strap and the stick, of course. They didn't need a reason to beat. Spare the rod and spoil the child, just as his aunt proclaimed. He had never been spared or spoiled.

When three older boys had cornered him one day, he had tried to walk away. He had no wish to hurt others and he knew how brutal the beating would be if one of the men in rough cloth caught him fighting. But they had left him no option. And by the time the boys had come to regret their decision to corner him and taunt him, it was too late. Two of the boys managed to get away with little more than bloodied noses. But one of them lay on his back, unmoving. His nose had been broken, two ribs fractured and his jaw dislocated. As the red mist cleared William realised he had wet himself. But not from fear.

He looked down at his disproportionately large hands, at the blood already beginning to dry on them, and then he looked up as he saw two men running angrily towards him.

The red mist came down again. In the end it took

three of them to restrain him. His body was battered and bruised before they took him into the room. There his trousers had been taken down and his bared backside had been strapped with cruel leather until blood was drawn.

He was eight years old.

Shortly after the incident he had been sent to a special school. A boarding school for troubled youth. Where discipline and exercise and moral guidance were supposed to forge a virtuous man from a miscreant youth. He was forged, sure enough. But into something hard, and brutal and vengeful.

They had kept him locked in an empty room for over three hours. When the key turned in the lock he looked across at the door and swallowed hard as it scraped open. He didn't regret what he had done to the boys – they had brought the fire down on their own heads – but he was aware that there would be consequences. One thing he knew now, though, was that although he had not wished to inflict pain on them, when his hand had been forced he'd found that he enjoyed it. He could have stopped but hadn't wanted to. It was as though something had been released within him, something that had defined him through blood. Whatever happened to him in the future, he decided, he'd make a pact with himself to repay it with interest. He looked down at the front of his urine-stained jeans and felt not shame but anger. A red flush rose in his cheeks as he clenched his fist and dug unclean and ragged nails into his palm.

The man who entered the room was Luke Carlow.

A forty-five-year-old unrepentant sodomiser of children. He had a degree in sociology and was the person in charge of the home for delinquent youth that William had been placed in. 'Delinquent', Carlow often thought, was such a quaint and ridiculous term for the criminal scum he had to deal with. Too young to be sent to a proper prison, they were kept segregated from the public to whom they were a threat. But they themselves were not protected from other men who might do them harm – men like Luke Carlow.

William was allowed to shower first before Carlow buggered him. Cleanliness is next to godliness, after all, and one thing Carlow couldn't abide was a filthy boy.

Later, curled up on his bed, William didn't cry. The bleeding was staining his sheets but he forced himself not to shed a single tear. Later still, when the older boy that he was forced to share a room with came in, he could see the look of appetite squirming in the other boy's eyes and knew that the ordeal was far from over.

Eight years on, Luke Carlow would be discovered dead inside a damp cubicle in a filthy public lavatory in King's Lynn. He was found with a pair of filth-stained underpants stuffed in his mouth. His penis had been severed with a pair of secateurs and he had been stabbed repeatedly in his throat.

The older boy who had shared that cell with the eight-year-old William would disappear and would never be found. Even if he had been, his own mother would not have been able to recognise him from the mass of mangled flesh to which he had been reduced.

9

I was lying on the doctor's examination couch.

My shirt had been unbuttoned, exposing my – if I say so myself – finely toned torso. I expected the lady doctor to be more impressed with my physique than she seemed to be, judging by the expression on her face as she probed my musculature with cool, slender fingers, her perfectly trimmed nails immaculately painted in postbox red.

'What the hell happened to you?' she asked. 'You look like someone took a baseball bat to your stomach!'

She had a point. I looked down at the bruising which was already beginning to turn a very unpleasant colour. 'Something very similar.'

I winced as her skilled hands probed and examined the area. 'Can you go a bit more gently with that?' I said.

'Go gently!' she said. 'You're lucky I don't kick your sorry Irish backside. What the hell happened?'

'There was a conflict of interest in a financial situation. Seemed that words were not sufficient to bring the other party to a negotiated settlement.'

I winced even more violently as she probed deliberately harder this time. 'OK! I was doing a favour for a friend.'

'What friend?'

'Amy, the solicitor. You've met her.'

'I hope she's paying you well is all I can say.'

'She puts a lot of work my way.'

'Maybe she does. But this isn't the sort of work that you, or I, or your family need,' she said pointedly.

'A couple of cowboy builders conned a sweet old lady out of some serious money and I asked them to return it.'

'And they objected?' she asked, unable to keep the sarcasm out of her voice.

'I am afraid they did, Kate darling.' I looked up at her beautiful face, framed with silken dark tresses, saw the passion sparking in her big luminous eyes and felt myself drowning in them all over again.

'Don't "darling" me! We came up to Norfolk to get away from the violence, or don't you remember that?'

'I had to do something.'

'It's not a doctor you should be seeing, Jack. It's a psychotherapist to help you with that white-knight syndrome of yours.'

I smiled and shrugged and the smile fell right off my face as my stomach muscles protested at the movement. That guy seriously had a punch like a mule's kick. Lucky for me he didn't know how to box. Often the way with big strong men who get their bulk from weightlifting or heavy manual labour. They're not used to people standing up to them. And when they do it's a strength contest, a war of attrition. They get knocked down, then they get up again. Only difference with me was that I knew how to punch and where. And I usually had the element of surprise on my side. I never wait to be asked to dance. If it's going down then you get yours in first. First and hard. My dad had taught me that much.

'She really is a dear old lady, quite a character. You'd like her,' I said as Kate continued with her probing, a little more gently this time.

'This "dear old lady" have a name?'

'Helen Middleton, no relation.'

Kate stood up and nodded. 'I know her. She's a patient here. You better make sure she is taken care of!' she said in her no-nonsense schoolteacher tone that I had become accustomed to.

I blinked at the volte-face. 'That's what I said!'

'I mean it. She's a lovely woman.'

Sometimes you have to just roll with the punches. 'Yes, dear.'

'Okay. You can take the shirt off now, Jack. Doesn't seem to be anything broken. Just bruising and tissue damage. It will hurt for a while. Try not to laugh too much or cough.'

'And how do I do that?' I asked as I took off my shirt.

'Force of will power.'

'And what are you going to do?'

'Bandage you up and give you some painkillers.'

'You could always prescribe a bottle of Jameson's – that's quite effective in the painkilling area.'

She pursed her lips. 'Co-codamol will be just fine.'

A few years back and I had what is technically called a drinking problem. Whiskey was my main poison of choice. I'd drink it till my brain and sensibilities had been anaesthetised, and the past and the future disappeared with every tumbler of the amber oblivion that I drank. Until, finally, all that was left was the cosy, hazy cotton-wool present. Laughter and noise and faces that I would never remember. Women I wouldn't recall. One-night stands or prostitutes I would take up against a brick wall or a garden fence, or down some darkened alleyway. Fighting and fornicating my way round Soho and Shepherd's Bush. A psychoanalyst would probably tell me it was guilt. A downwardly spiralling vicious circle of self-loathing and disgust. The whiskey didn't just take away the pain of simply living, it took me away from myself. For a few hours I could forget who I was, and become something worse.

My pregnant wife had died when I had intervened in an armed robbery at a petrol station. Goodness knows what I was thinking of at the time. She took the shotgun blast which was aimed at me and she died a short while later in hospital, and my baby that she was carrying died with her. I had another child, a daughter. Siobhan. But rather than keeping it together and looking after her I carried on working and drinking and pretty much destroyed myself.

Another woman's death was the catalyst for change, as they say. Not a woman I loved in the traditional sense of the word. A woman I had made love to, though, and more than once. An Irish woman, like me an exile from the land of her birth. Jackie Moiyne – she had dark curling locks as a gift from her marooned Spanish forebears who'd been washed up on the south shore of Ireland when their invading Armada fell foul of the English weather that saved Drake's bacon. And she had flashing blue eyes that bespoke of the gypsy nature of her soul.

Jackie Moiyne was a prostitute and while I might not have loved her I liked her. I liked her a lot. When she was murdered it should have been enough to sober me up and sort out my life: she had deserved my full attention as lead detective on the case and I figured I had owed her that much. But I let her down – or I would have done if Kate Walker hadn't also got involved. She was the forensic pathologist assigned to the case and we were thrown into a working relationship which, as sometimes happens, strayed into the personal. I had never thought I would love again, but I was wrong.

I discovered that Kate had skeletons in her closet, too. An uncle who was a senior member of the Metropolitan Police, and who had abused her in childhood, turned out to be linked to the murder. A group of men were taking runaway children off the street. Using them in a large house in Henley-on-Thames. Using, abusing, photographing them and filming it all. Jackie's brother had also been involved and when her son went missing it was that that prompted her murder. Her brother was murdered too when he tried to blackmail Kate's uncle.

When my own child had been taken, Kate's help had been crucial in getting her back safely and putting her uncle and his associates behind bars for a very long time. I had rescued my daughter but in the process Dr Kate Walker had rescued me, too. I owed her my life. Everything.

It was Kate who saved me.

She spoke, snapping me out of my reverie, and I felt a chill pass over my heart as I registered her words.

'We need to talk, Jack.'

We need to talk.

Probably the most unpleasant arrangement of four simple words in the world.

'Go on?' I said, swinging my legs over the examination couch to the floor and buttoning my shirt back up over the bandage that Kate had applied.

'The wedding, Jack! We need to talk about the wedding.'

I sighed with relief. 'Plenty of time for that, darling. It's not until next year. Let's talk it through tonight at home. When you're not so busy.'

'I've tried talking to you at home, but you never sit still long enough to make any decisions.'

'You know what my decision would be. We'd fly off to the Caribbean, just the four of us, and get married on the beach. Come home as Mr and Mrs Jack Delaney with none of the associated hullabaloo.'

'We are not running off anywhere, Jack. I hope you're not ashamed of me.'

'Of course I'm not!'

'Then you should be prepared to declare your love

for me in front of the whole world! That's what marriage is all about after all, isn't it?'

Kate had a way of dancing me into corners with her words. Questions that I couldn't answer without being in the wrong. 'Are you sure you never trained as a lawyer?'

'I'm being serious!'

I stood up and kissed her. But her lips remained closed tight and the glint in her eye was not one of mischief, but a warning of dark clouds gathering therein.

'I've said I am happy to get married here, didn't I? We've set the date and picked the church. Church of England at that!'

'You don't have to sound like you are doing me a favour!'

'Well, we can't get married in a Catholic church and you don't want a registrar performing the ceremony.'

'Don't you play the Catholic card on me, Jack Delaney!' she snapped. Seemed I was right about the gathering clouds.

'Well, I was just saying.'

'You are never "just saying" anything. I know you well enough by now for that.'

'You know I love you and just want to make you happy.'

'And that's why you're marrying me?'

I could see it was a loaded question because of the challenging look in her eyes. 'Of course not,' I said. Trying to work out quickly what trap she had set. 'I'm marrying you because it would make me the happiest and luckiest man in Christendom.'

Her look softened. Perhaps I'd danced around the landmine this time.

'And you really mean that?'

'Sure, if I were to lie to you would not my tongue blacken and fall from my mouth?'

Kate laughed despite herself. 'I must be all kinds of fool to be marrying you, Jack.'

'It doesn't matter what kind of fool – you're *my* fool and that's all that matters.'

She looked at me, considering for a moment, and then smiled again. 'Yes,' she said. 'Yes, it is.'

'OK. I'd better report back to Amy.'

'You are going nowherc!' Hcr voiced snapped back into schoolteacher mode. 'I told Lesley to hold all appointments for the next half an hour.' She pulled a fat folder out of a drawer. 'There is plenty to arrange. Wedding music. Guest lists. The wedding-breakfast menu. Flowers for the church and the reception. Wedding invitations. Wedding stationery. Honeymoon destinations. I have booked the village hall in Upper Sheringham, but we need to talk about entertainment. Bridal car for me. Car for you and your party.'

'Yes, dear.' I summoned up a smile from somewhere. That beach on Barbados was looking far more attractive by the minute.

'And what if it rains?' She continued.

'Umbrellas?

Kate didn't even bother to respond. 'And your best man . . . have you picked someone yet?'

'I thought Sally Cartwright.'

'Think again. Much as I love that detective

constable I want a traditional wedding and not some other woman standing beside you at the altar making bookends of us both.'

'Yes, dear.'

'And if you call me "dear" one more time I am going to pick up my reflex hammer and brain you with it.'

11

An hour later and I was sitting back in the caravan, nursing a bruised stomach and a bottle of Fullers Honeydew beer, watching a stable girl walk across the yard to the farmhouse.

Jodhpurs, riding boots, a green waterproof jacket, long blonde hair tied back in a shaggy ponytail. Time was, I would have invited her into the caravan to join me for a drink. I wasn't even considering it now. Well, not seriously. But a man's eye is drawn to the female figure as a moth is drawn to a flame, as some poet might have remarked once. I took another sip of my beer and smiled inwardly. I may still shoot the occasional glance but I had no desire to act. I wasn't lying when I said I loved Kate. Everything had changed with her.

Like I said, I used to hate the taste of real ale. Maybe they served it differently down south but since moving to the North Norfolk Coast I had acquired a taste for it. Maybe my metabolism was changing. Probably some science in it – I would ask Kate but she'd only make me laugh and I was forbidden to do that. Maybe it was just because most people round here drank it, including a many the women. When in Rome drink like a Roman. Kate thought it was part of a psychological shift, a metaphorical putting-down of roots. I reminded her that she had qualifications in medicine and forensics, not in psychology or psychiatry, and she had simply smiled at me in a way she had that made me feel too good about her to be irritated. Who knows, maybe she was right. In the cold winter nights at the farthest outpost of civilisation, with nothing between me and the North Pole except thousands of miles of hostile sea, there was something comforting about sitting in front of a real fire in an old pub, listening to the wind howl and drinking something that had its roots in the first intoxicating beverages made by man.

I looked out of the other window, the one at the far end of the caravan, at a herringbone sky flecked with veins of crimson as the weak sun dipped towards the horizon. Halloween would soon be upon us and then Bonfire Night and looking at that sky I felt the power of forces that shaped the personality of this landscape and its people. A pagan power rooted in flame and ceremony, dating from long, long before the birth of Christ. I took another pull on my Honeydew ale and shook my head, smiling wryly. Saints alive, sure I'd be drinking mead next. I put the bottle down as the door opened and a woman walked in without waiting for an invitation.

She was in her late thirties, maybe mid-forties. I may be a detective, but what with Botox and fillers and who knows what monkey-gland elixirs nowadays

I sure as hell wouldn't like to stake my life on making a completely accurate guess at a woman's age. Bad manners, too. She had brunette hair, cut short in a Louise Brooks-style bob, and wore a dark charcoal dress suit whose hem came just above her shapely knees. She had great pins. Like I said before, moth to flame and all that, but in my defence I *am* a detective – I am paid to notice these things. She was a good-looking woman and knew it. She wasn't shy about make-up but it was subtly applied, although her lipstick was a cherry red that accentuated the blueness of her eyes, eyes that were looking at me with a degree of confidence that signalled she was used to getting her own way. I could see a lot of men would be happy to do her bidding. She was a snap-her-fingers-and-see-them-run kind of woman. She exuded sex, confidence, authority. She wasn't wearing a wedding ring.

Maybe this time she would say 'I've come to see you, Mister Delaney, because I think some men have been following me.' In a husky whisper just like Marilyn Monroe's in some 1950s film noir whose title I forget.

'What the fuck are you playing at, Delaney?' she said instead, exploding my flights of fancy.

'Afternoon, Susan,' I replied giving her the benefit of the full wattage of my smile. 'How's your day going?' The full wattage had no effect on her. Her eyes remained as hard as the bark on a frozen tree.

'That's Superintendent Dean to you. And my day was going fine until a certain pain in the arse of an Irishman got in the woodpile.'

'Something amiss?' I asked innocently.

'I just had a man in my police station accusing one of my officers of endangering his life and assaulting his mentally challenged colleague.'

I shrugged. 'What's that got to do with me?'

'That's a bloody good question, Delaney!'

She didn't pronounce my name with any particular relish.

'I am certain that if one of your men acted in a forceful way,' I said, 'he was perfectly justified. I know you run a very tidy ship up here, Susan. A very tidy ship.'

'Don't get funny, Delaney. Your brogue and your supposed Irish diddly bloody charm might have had the ladies in Paddington Green dropping their knickers, but you fuck around with me and I will come down on you like a ton of proverbial bricks. A veritable shitstorm!'

'Do you kiss your mother with those lips?' I asked, pretending to be shocked at her language. 'And you're mixing your metaphors there.'

'Shut it, Delaney. And tell me what the hell you were doing assaulting a couple of law-abiding members of my community? And don't try bullshitting me. Bill Collier gave me a perfectly good description of you. What makes you think you can get away with flashing a warrant card and pretending to be on the force?'

'Technically, Susan, I *am* still on the force.'

'Not my bloody force you're not! And you're on sabbatical, last I heard. From the Met. You want to take up policing again, rather than poncing about interfering with matters that don't concern you, why don't you sod off back to the big city and do it there?'

'I only went to have a quiet chat with the man. It was his colleague who started it.'

'Who started it! What are you? Twelve years old, for God's sake?'

'They defrauded an old lady out of a lot of money. They are not law-abiding citizens, they are a pair of shifty, sleazy, cowboy conmen.'

'Then that is a civil matter. It is *not* a police matter and certainly not one where you can go round flashing a warrant card pretending to be part of my team.'

'I never said I was part of your team.'

'You implied it and that is as good in my eyes. Do it again I will have you in the nick so fast your head will spin. I don't care if you're a Met officer taking a gap year or not. This is my patch. Trust me,' she said, with a cold smile. 'Don't be looking for any preferential treatment from me.'

I flashed her a smile of my own. 'You come all the way out here in person to tell me this, superintendent?'

'Don't flatter yourself. I have a meeting scheduled with the vicar up the road on parish-council business. Just consider yourself told.'

She turned on her high heels and opened the door.

'Yes, ma'am!' I said with military crispness.

She turned back to glare at me but settled for slamming the door behind her as a parting comment.

I picked up my bottle of beer and finished what was left. 'Still got it, Cowboy,' I said to myself. 'Still got it.'

I looked around the trailer and then at the telephone on the desk. I thought about recording a new message saying, 'This is Jack Delaney. At the tone leave your name and message. I'll get back to you.'

Instead, I looked at my watch, then out at the sky that was dark now. I placed my empty beer bottle into the waste-paper basket by my desk as a crack of lightning rang out like a rifle shot. A few seconds later and an angry rumble of thunder swept in from the coast, and a few seconds after that the heavens opened up and the rain hammering on the metal roof of the caravan became almost deafening once again. I shrugged into my overcoat, pulled on a baseball cap and braved the weather. I had to be brave, after all – it was in my job description.

12

Night-time in the city.

Warm hazy air. Smells of petrol and industrial output mingling with the aromatic smoke of barbecues wafting from back gardens here and there. Yellow light pooling on the ground from sulphurous street lamps. Neon signs flashing. The distant wail of a police siren and an ambulance siren in cacophonous disharmony. Cars flashing past in both directions. Another city that rarely sleeps. Cigarette smoke drifting out of the open car window. Minutes later I pulled the car hard left and parked. Switching off the engine but keeping the radio on.

I stood for a while, my eyes half-closed. The Cowboy Junkies were playing 'Blue Moon' now. Soulful. The hot night like a moist, warm blanket. Airless. I could feel beads of sweat forming on my forehead.

I holstered the petrol-pump nozzle back in its cradle and turned round to see Eddie Bonner standing there. He had a smart suit on, his shirt was buttoned up and neatly ironed, and he was wearing a silk tie in dark colours. But he looked haunted. His troubled brown eyes flicked nervously as he watched me, then they steadied with purpose. A cold purpose, as if he had come to a decision. He held a shotgun in his right hand. He lifted it up and held the barrel with his left hand as he pointed it at me. I felt the beads of sweat trickle down from my forehead onto the bridge of my nose and into my eyes. I blinked to keep the moisture away.

I held a hand up in a placating gesture. But the younger man shook his head, almost apologetically.

'Whatever it is, Eddie, we can work it out.'

'It's too late for that, Jack. Far too late.'

'It's never too late.'

'We're all born with a use-by date, sir. It's part of the deal.'

'You don't have to call me "sir". We're friends, aren't we, Eddie?'

'We were never friends. But I guess you never did understand that, did you? You being the hotshot detective and all, I would have thought you would have worked that out long ago. Maybe your gut instincts aren't all they are cracked up to be.'

'And maybe they are. You don't want this, Eddie. I can see it in your eyes.'

'Like I say, Jack, it's too late. Far too late for any of us.'

I held my hand forward again. 'I don't understand this.'

'It's all about checks and balances. You crossed a line, Cowboy. You messed up big time and somebody has to pay. You think running away from London changes any of that? At the end of the day someone has to pay. Someone always does.'

'I did what I had to do.'

Bonner raised the shotgun and levelled it at my stomach. 'You better say your goodbyes.'

Before I could reply he had pulled the trigger. The blast was like a burning iron fist in my gut. I cried out in pain, spun round and dropped to my knees. The shot had passed straight through me. My wife, with an extremely swollen pregnant belly, was standing holding her hands to her shattered stomach. Blood was running through her fingers in rivulets. She had taken the full force of both barrels. She too fell to her knees and smiled sadly at me. Her eyes were peaceful and she seemed to be in no pain, but large tears welled after a second.

'It's all right, Jack,' she said. 'Take care of Siobhan for me.' And then her eyes closed and the alarm rang out, blanking out the sounds of my screams. So that all I could hear was the roar of blood in my ears and the knelling of bells.

I started awake, my eyes wet with tears.

My hand fumbled in the dark for the mobile phone on the cabinet beside the bed. Kate switched on her bedside lamp as I picked up the phone and then dropped it again. My hands were shaking so much.

'What is it, Jack?' she asked.

'I'll be OK. Let me get this.' I pushed the button on the phone. 'Delaney. This had better be good!' I said.

'It's not good I'm afraid, Jack.'

'Henry?' I rubbed a hand over my eyes, trying to clear my head.

'Sorry to wake you up so early and please apologise to your lovely wife for me. Had no choice, I am afraid. It's an all-hands-to-the-pump kind of situation.'

Henry Hill was the secretary of Sheringham Golf club and had employed me on retainer as a security consultant for them.

I looked at the clock. It was ten to six. 'That's okay, Henry. What's up? A break-in?' I said, looking down at my left hand. It had stopped shaking, and I wiped my sweat-beaded forehead with it.

'Part of the cliff has collapsed in the night. It was a very heavy storm.'

'Yeah, I know. Whereabouts?'

'A considerable landslide on the walkway bordering the sixth fairway. Well, I say "fairway". Technically, considering it is a par three, it doesn't have a fairway—'

'That's OK, Henry, I know where you mean,' I said, cutting him off before he started quoting the rules and regulations from the Royal and Ancient handbook. 'What do you want me to do?'

'Get out here. Like I said, we need all hands on deck. We have to seal off the area. The public footpath went down with the cliff, so we can't have people walking on the golf course and taking a tumble eighty feet or more down to the beach.'

'Not a good idea, no. I'll be there as soon as possible.' I clicked the phone off and turned to Kate.

'Sorry about that.'

She put her hand on my forehead. 'What's up, Jack? You're all clammy and you were making noises in your sleep.'

'I'm OK.'

'Was it the dream again?'

'Worse this time. Bonner was there with a double-barrelled shotgun and he blasted both barrels into her stomach. And she was swollen, Kate. Past-full-term swollen.'

She held my hand sympathetically.

I swallowed. 'A few days' time and it will be the anniversary of the due date we were given for the birth.'

Kate pulled me into a hug and I let her. Burying my face in her soft dark curls. Taking comfort from smelling her hair, feeling her hot breath, the warmth of her body. Her vitality.

'Maybe that's why it's on your mind just lately.'

'I guess so.'

'It will get better. The dreams will go.'

'I know,' I said, not entirely believing it to be true and feeling guilty that I should wish away memories of my dead wife, however grotesque and warped they were in the dream.

'What's the crisis at the golf club?'

'Some of the cliff by the sixth hole has collapsed. Taking the public walkway with it.'

'Anybody hurt?'

'No. Don't think so. The coastguard just alerted us. They had a call come in from someone out walking his dog. An ex-copper, apparently. He always goes out early before the golfers get there and order him off their private land. Not that there would be anyone playing today.'

'I shouldn't think so.'

'Luckily for our dog-walker the storm had cleared the clouds for a while and the moon was out, otherwise he might not have seen the danger.'

'It's about time the government did something about it, Jack. People are losing their homes, entire villages have gone, and they still let it happen.'

'Might as well wish for the moon to be blue, with cows jumping over it, as expect that lot to do anything unless they've got a vested interest. I'll try and be back for breakfast.'

'Sure,' Kate said and kissed me again. I could see little worry creases in the corners of her eyes as she nibbled a thumbnail distractedly, watching me as I got out of bed and dressed in a rush.

13

It was still dark.

Seven o'clock and there was just the merest hint of light breaking among the dark clouds to the east.

I had a watch cap on, my thermal T, a shirt and my black leather jacket. Like a divvy I had left my overcoat at home and it was cold out there on the cliff's edge. I flapped my arms around myself to warm up a little. It didn't seem to do much good. I still hesitated, however, as Henry Hill held out a large silver hip flask to me. But not for long. I opened it and took a nip. It was sweet.

'Cherry brandy?' I asked, surprised.

Henry Hill smiled. He was a man of medium height, with sandy hair and a neat moustache. A stickler for details, procedures and protocol. Which was fitting as Sheringham Golf Club was an old-fashioned club. Been going since Victoria was alive. I had a sneaking suspicion that they would have had a men-only bar if they could have got away with it.

A large number of people had gathered on the clifftops, all wearing hi-vis vests over overcoats and warm clothing. There was a kind of Blitz spirit in the air, the community coming together to deal with a local disaster if not exactly a tragedy. The thunderstorm that had raged in the night had passed but, like I said, it was still cold enough to freeze the legendary tits off a witch in a brass brassiere, as my da always used to say. Not in my ma's hearing he didn't say it, mind. He wasn't that brave.

Sheringham Golf Club is a weird beast. Some claim it is a links course, and links are traditionally where the strips of land lie before you reach the beach and the shoreline proper. Which was true here, but the parts of the course closest to the beach here are on the clifftops beside it. This means it's an elevated course, eighty feet above sea level in places. So some would claim it is not a true links course. Personally I don't know enough about the game to be able to tell, and favour your man's opinion that 'a game of golf is a good walk spoiled'. You can certainly see the sea to some extent from all but one of the holes on a good day. On the north side of the course there are the cliff edges, where we were gathered, and the course itself is sandwiched between them and the tracks of the Poppy Line steam railway which runs from the old Sheringham station through to the equally old stations of Weybourne and Holt. A big tourist attraction in the season, and the views and the sight of the old steam engines pulling old carriages make a fine sight when the sun is out.

Standing out of season by the tee on the sixth hole, however, with the North Sea thundering below and the winds biting like evil and ancient Scandinavian spirits, it wasn't quite so awfully jolly. Henry offered me another nip of the cherry brandy, which I did not decline. He gestured over as a man was allowed through the human cordon, ducking under the POLICE – DO NOT CROSS tape which been set up around a large area of the sixth hole and the fifth green. The flapping tape didn't look too effective to me as a measure for crowd control. Luckily there weren't any crowds and neither were they expected. The holiday-makers were away and the locals had seen enough coastal erosion and cliff slide in the past to stop them venturing out in this kind of foul weather.

'Martin Lewis,' said Henry Hill as he indicated the man who was walking towards us. 'Geological boffin reporting to the North Norfolk Council.'

He looked as much like a scientist as I looked like a cup cake. He was about five foot four high and just about the same wide. In his mid to late thirties, at a guess. He might have had the long hair of the mad professor, I'd give him that, but his was dyed black and shaved at the temples. He was wearing a long leather coat and Celtic tattoos were quite visible on both wrists. A Geogoth, perhaps. I couldn't see him listening to Mahler. Motorhead, maybe. But then, I have been wrong about people in the past.

'Hello, Henry,' he said as he strolled up, smiling broadly and displaying a very well maintained and very white set of teeth. 'Been landscaping your course, I hear.'

'Someone has but I fear it is the hand of God, not mine. This is Jack Delaney,' he said, gesturing at me.

The scientist held out his own hand and since there was no lightning bolt leaping from his fingers I shook it. 'What's happening, bro?' he asked.

I shrugged. 'I wouldn't have a clue. Not my area of expertise.'

Henry Hill left me to show Lewis the extent of the landslide. From the sixth tee we could see the fresh scars, as a twenty-foot-or-more-wide chunk of cliff had sheared off all the way down to the shoreline, leaving a heap of debris weighing many, many tonnes piled up on the beach. The landfall rising in a central mound like the remains of a sand sculpture of an enormous beached whale after the sea and the wind had been at it.

'You can see the strata quite clearly defined in the cliff face now, Jack,' said Martin Lewis, pointing out the exposed variations in colour and the various visible composite materials as the cliff rose higher. 'Bit like a layer cake.'

'And that makes it more liable to collapse, does it?'

'Can do – depends what the elements are. But, in this case, yes – and certainly liable to slower erosion. That is more common along these shores than this kind of large-scale fissuring,' he said, pointing animatedly. 'There is a chalk base at the bottom of the cliff which you can see quite clearly and resting above that are what we call the Lower Pleistocene deposits of the Pastonian stage. These cliffs were formed many thousands of years ago by glacial deposits from the last ice age.'

'The one we are still in, apparently.'

'Yes, well done.' He nodded approvingly. I was beginning to feel like I might need to put my hand up to ask a question. 'That is technically so. The glacial movement from the north made landfall here and stopped. You can see the sections of the glacial deposits here.' He pointed again. 'And this is known as the Contorted Drift.'

'Which makes it unstable?' I asked, guessing.

'The glacial progress churned up everything in its way and what you see here is a kind of geological cake mix. Add in chalk and sand and you get a truly variegated structure. But having a chunk this size just shear off is very uncommon. The chalk base is a sturdy one. Think of the white cliffs of Dover, for example.'

I nodded, mainly thinking about Vera Lynn but I didn't reckon that was what he was hinting at. 'There was some speculation that a lightning strike might have been the cause?' I prompted.

'It's possible. There can be a lot of energy in a lightning bolt.'

'How much?'

Lewis smiled. 'It's more than enough to fry an egg, that's for sure. But larger bolts of lightning can transfer up to one hundred and twenty thousand amperes and deliver a kick of three hundred and fifty coulombs.'

'What's a coulomb?'

'It's the electrical charge at the rate of one ampere delivered in one second.'

'So that's definitely a lot?' Physics and maths were never my long suits.

'Oh yes. With a positively charged lightning bolt it might have originated several miles away in the storm. Travelling through the air for that distance enables the positively charged part to develop larger levels of charge and voltages.'

'So now we really *are* talking about a lot of energy?'

'Yes, we are. Your positive bolt can be up to ten times more powerful than your negative bolt. The potential for the positive bolt from the anvil at the top of the cloud formation could go over a billion volts and the discharge current, or the amount of time during which the bolt transfers that energy from the charged cloud to the ground below, can go on for ten times longer than a negative transfer.'

I nodded encouragingly. I didn't really need all the technical jargon but in my job you learn to let people talk. It's the listening that counts. Often people don't know what they know, as it were. 'So to sum it up, this partial cliff collapse could be the result of a lightning strike, possibly a positive-charged one?'

The scientist shrugged, his long hair swirling in the wind. 'Could be. Like I say, we are dealing with a lot of energy. But if it struck at the top, here by the pathway, or even halfway up, there would be no reason for the cliff to shear all the way down. It's possible with a vertical fault line. Normally If there is a landslide it is just from the top, and it produces nowhere near this amount of debris.'

'What about if it struck at the bottom?'

'It wouldn't do that – it finds the nearest point to

strike. Literally earthing itself, in this case. That's the nature of the beast. It finds the higher ground.'

'That's true.' I knew that much about lightning. People still get killed on golf courses because they hold long metal lightning conductors called irons and swing them up in the air during thunderstorms. Go figure. Darwin's theory of survival of the fittest, maybe, as a practical demonstration.

The geologist looked over the cliff again and smiled. 'It sure is a puzzler,' he said.

'What are the implications for the course?'

'None, I should think. This looks like a one-off occurrence – if there is some kind of fault line we can soon establish if it's continuing, but I haven't come across such a thing around here. I should imagine there is enough cliff edge here to establish the pathway again without encroaching on the course. May have to swing round a little but not enough to impact on your fairway.'

'It's a par three,' I said. 'You don't have fairways on par threes.'

Nobody can say I'm not a quick learner.

'I'm not a golfer,' Lewis said dryly, knowing that he certainly didn't look like one.

'You say it's a puzzler?'

'It is that.'

'Could it have been deliberate?'

'What do you mean?'

'Somebody bringing down the cliff. Setting off an explosive device.'

'Why on Earth would anybody want to do that?'

I shrugged. 'I don't know. It's just my job to ask questions like that,' I replied. 'I'm trained mainly to look out for human wickedness in unexplained situations where people have come to harm or property has been damaged.'

He gave me a curious look. 'As a security consultant?'

'I used to be a detective inspector in the Metropolitan Police,' I explained.

'Ah, I see.' Lewis looked thoughtfully at the collapsed section of cliff on the beach where it stretched out like a huge and ancient burial barrow. 'Like I said, I can see no reason why anybody would want to do such a thing,' he stated, looking at me steadily. 'But yes – it is entirely possible that this collapse is the work of some human agency.'

14

The sun had risen now.

It was shining weakly through the ragged remnants of clouds that hadn't been ravaged by the north-westerly wind. A wind which had come screaming in once more from the North Sea to punish us lowly mortal men and women scurrying on the surface of the Earth. The sky was a light, almost silvery grey and the sun creeping through was pale rose in colour and struggling to brighten. It wasn't any warmer.

I was holding a large styrofoam cup of coffee in one hand and chatting with some of the hi-vis-coated men and women who had been posted at the barricade, such as it was. The heavy-metal-fan-cum-council-geologist had gone down on the shore to take some samples and assess the situation further. There was a cordon of tape still stretched all around the danger area up on the clifftop where we were standing. A mixture of uniformed police, club personnel and a few members had been drafted in, making sure that no curious people got too close to the landslide edge. I was keeping an eye out for my old pal Henry and his good friend the cherry-brandy hip flask, but as I looked back towards the clubhouse I saw a different yet still familiar face bearing down on me. It was a good-looking face, but not a happy one. Superintendent Susan Dean had a man of about five foot eleven walking alongside her who was wearing a brown suit with a duffel coat over it. A briefcase was in his hand, and he had a very officious look about him.

'Delaney!' said the super.

'Susan, always a pleasure,' I replied.

'Henry Hill says I am to speak to you.'

'Regarding?'

'The cost of baked bloody beans. What do you think!' she asked rhetorically and pointed over to the cliff edge.

'Well, I can tell you all about the cliff composition, the chalk base, et cetera. It's all to do with the start of the ice age and the glacial migration,' I said.

'What?'

'Something to do with the plasticine era,' I continued, suppressing a smile. 'Which made a kind of layer cake of the cliff's substructure, apparently. But I can't tell you why such a large chunk fell. Apparently it happens sometimes. A metre a year in some cases where there's gradual erosion, but occasionally there is a bit of a landslide. My geological friend down on the beach there,' I said, pointing at Martin Lewis, 'agrees that a lightning strike might have caused a bit of an explosion, if you will, causing a shearing of the varied fabric of the cliff that resulted in the toppling forward of that bit thus separated.'

'Are you deliberately trying to be obtuse?'

'Not at all. It's not my area of expertise. But I'm just trying to do my job, Susan. Like everyone else.'

'It's "superintendent" or "ma'am" to you, Delaney.'

I smiled and shook my head tolerantly. 'You can't have it both ways,' I said. 'If I am not on the force you can't expect me to jump to heel like an obedient dog. If I am a member of the public I deserve just as much respect and courtesy as anyone else,' I said and flashed her another smile for good measure. I wasn't having the best of mornings so far, so I took what small comforts I could to brighten my day.

'I don't have time for this bullshit, Delaney. Some of us have proper work to do.' She glared at me as she said the word 'proper', and looked ready to spit. 'I'll leave you to deal with this,' she said to the man who had come over with her and then she walked off. Letting the world know just how extremely busy she was as she did so with head held high and a purposeful stride. She almost managed it if her heel hadn't snagged a little on the rough grass and she nearly tripped over. Like I say, small moments, small comforts.

The man held his hand out. 'Nicholas Dudley,' he said.

'Jack Delaney.' I shook his hand.

'Health and Safety consultant to the district council. We have some issues here that we need to go through.'

'Right,' I said, my heart sinking as he pulled out a folder.

'First of all we need to erect appropriate barriers to safeguard the public.'

'Sure.'

'And we need to close this club down until we have a proper geological survey and report.'

I looked up at the dark clouds that were massing ominously in the sky as the wind lashed the sea into a frenzy of dancing white horses. I felt the cold permeating through to my bones, finished my styrofoam cup of coffee, and looked at Dudley. 'Are you fucking serious?' I asked.

'One hundred per cent serious. I know a lot of people think health-and-safety regulations are just so much red tape and needless bureaucracy. But we are dealing with people's lives, Mr Delaney. People's lives! And we take that very seriously. Very seriously indeed.'

'Do you really think people are going to want to go out and play golf in this weather? Nobody is that mad, even in North Norfolk!'

'It's not about madness, it's about regulations. It's about securing the safety of the public. This club will be closed until further notice. Furthermore, I have a checklist that I need to go through with you. It will probably take a couple of hours, and the geological specialist will be consulting with me later in the day, so we will need to evaluate matters again after he has reported, too.'

I was beginning to understand why Henry Hill had passed this particular buck to me, and why the bustling superintendent had had a wry smile on her perfectly lipsticked lips as she had strode away.

'Why don't we go inside and go through it?'

'No, no. I need to assess the area before then.

Health and Safety is a field operation first and fore-most, Mr Delaney. Sure, there is a lot of paperwork involved. But we as a profession are very far from desk jockeys. Very far indeed.'

I could feel myself losing the will to live with every passing second that I spent in Dudley's company. I was relieved to see Henry Hill running up the short hill to where we were stood. Until I saw the expression on his face, that was.

'Don't worry about him now, Jack,' he said breathlessly.

'Now hold on a minute—'

'Why, what's happened?' I cut across the health-and-safety officer, interrupting him before he got into full flow again.

'They've found a dead body.'

15

The wind was picking up by the second as we stood on the beach. An excoriating wind. I decided it was time to go home and get my overcoat: the leather jacket alone just wasn't cutting it in this climate.

Maybe I was just getting old.

Fortunately, Henry Hill came across and handed me a Puffa-style coat that would fit over my own. It was warm and cut the wind-chill factor significantly. Gratefully, I slipped my hands into a pair of gloves that he'd also brought and bent down to look at the body. Or, rather, at the hand that was protruding from the fall of soil and clay.

A uniformed sergeant was standing with us, a couple of constables in the background.

'This is a bit outside of our bailiwick, sir,' said the sergeant, a beefy florid-faced man in his forties with thinning reddish hair and friendly green eyes.

'You don't have to call me "sir",' I replied. 'I'm on sabbatical and, as your super has pointed out, not on her team.'

'I'll call you "sir" all the same, if that's OK?' he replied. 'We all know who you are. We read the newspapers and watch the news even out here in the sticks.'

'Newspapers exaggerate.'

'Sometimes. But I was on the force when you found the girl in the boot all those years ago and then again last year, when you repeated the trick.'

'Right place, right time is all.'

'You make your own luck in my opinion. Certainly in this job. And don't pay the super any mind. She doesn't like hot rods from the Met coming up. Puts her nose out of joint. She thinks that you all reckon you're something special. You in particular, with all that media coverage.'

I stood up again and held my hand out. 'Well, you know who I am,' I said, prompting him.

'Sergeant Coker – pleased to meet you,' he responded. 'Harry Coker.'

He was about my height but built on grander lines. His grip was very firm. His ruddy portliness belied a great deal of strength – there was a lot of muscle underneath his bulk.

'So what do you think?' he asked.

I looked down at the protruding hand again. We were on the beach close to the cliff face, the lifeless hand reaching up through the debris like the scene from *Carrie*, only this hand looked male to me. It was a big hand. Gloved. Part of the wrist was showing, discoloured and emaciated.

'Looks male to me. Maybe attached to a body, hard to tell until SOCO can clear the area. Do you have a forensic unit?'

The sergeant laughed and shook his head. 'No. Like I say, this is outside our normal remit. Dead bodies don't tend to show up a lot in these parts. We have to call in specialist units from South Norwich.'

'Well, he looks like a big man, judging by the hand size, although his emaciated wrist indicates malnourishment. Apart from that, and the discolouration, not much I can add.'

'How long has he been there, do you think?'

I shrugged. 'Again, hard to tell. These conditions.' I gestured towards the lowering storm that was building a few miles out to sea and heading our way.

'You think he was on the beach when the cliff collapsed?'

'It seems likely. But I have learned one thing over the years and that is never to assume too much until the experts have assessed the site and the body.'

I crouched down to get another look.

'Get away from the scene, Delaney!' barked a familiar voice.

I stood up and looked at the superintendent. She had arrived in her usual good temper, I noted.

'I asked him to take a look, ma'am,' said Sergeant Coker.

'And why the bloody hell would you do such a stupid thing?'

'Because he's a homicide detective. He has experience of these things, which we don't. And until the team from Norwich gets here I thought it might help to have all hands on deck.'

'That's my decision to make, sergeant.'

'When *are* the forensic surgeon and his team going to get here, ma'am?' he asked pointedly.

She looked annoyed at the question and didn't bother to hide it. 'They're not, sergeant. Not until tomorrow, anyway, and maybe not even then. There has been a major incident in the city. A fire set deliberately by the looks of it. Possibly a multiple murder and our one accidental death doesn't take priority.'

'If it was accidental,' I said.

'A cliff fell on him, Delaney. That's pretty hard to arrange deliberately.'

'I might be able to help,' I replied.

'I've already told you. We don't need or want your help.'

'It wasn't me I was thinking of.'

'What did you mean, then?' asked the sergeant, seemingly oblivious to the basilisk-like stare his boss was giving him.

'Doctor Walker, my fiancée, is a fully qualified and registered forensic pathologist. She can liaise with Norwich and help with a preliminary assessment so we know what we are dealing with here.'

I could see the superintendent chewing it over in her mind. She sure as hell didn't want to lose face by accepting any help from me, but it was a fair offer and she knew that she would be foolish to turn it down.

'The main thing we need to do is to get the site preserved. We need scene-of-crime tents securing the area – and quick – before the weather sets in again.'

The super looked at the size of the cliff fall and

sighed. 'We haven't got anything big enough. How soon can your wife clear authority with Norwich and get out here? We need to get this body moved as soon as possible.'

I looked at the storm getting ever closer and shrugged. 'I'm not sure. But I do know a man who used to have a marquee-hire business, with tents big enough for weddings and very large events. I am sure he can get a team down here soonest.'

'Get on it, then!' she ordered.

'Oh no, my pleasure,' I replied sardonically and pulled out my phone. 'You're very welcome, super-intendent. George, it's Jack Delaney,' I said as the phone was answered. 'I need a favour.'

16

About two hours later the storm finally made landfall at Sheringham, smiting the coastline like Thor's legendary hammer.

Fortunately George Bishop, the landlord at The Lobster public house, had come through and erected a marquee over the area where the dead body was situated, surrounded by broken-up chunks of chalk, as well as rock, shingle and sand. George had had the forethought to bring extra strong long steel pegs to be hammered into the shore. Happily the tide was a neap one and not a spring tide so it didn't come as high on this part of the beach and reach the cliff edges as it did closer into town. But I wasn't entirely sure how long the marquee would stay up in the battering wind. Not very long, though: the spikes might have been sturdy but a rock and pebble beach is not the best place to try and anchor something. The rain was falling in sheets and the noise under the big tent's canvas was close to tropical monsoon level.

Bright floodlights had been erected and a freelance SOCO team had been brought in to process the removal of the body. Most people assume that SOCO are all serving police officers but in reality there are a number of private firms that are called in sometimes to consult with the police. As the Norwich teams were already deployed on other business the superintendent had hired a private contractor. Two photographers were recording the scene. One was taking stills and the other had his camera mounted on a tripod and was shooting video. If it was a non-accidental death and the case ever came to trial then the evidence collected at the scene of the crime could be crucial to a successful prosecution, so meticulous care had to be taken. And they were certainly being meticulous. A lot of crime-solving is like that. Methodical procedure. Hour after hour of painstaking investigation. Not my favourite part of the job, but that's why a DI is given constables and sergeants. Thankfully.

Kate had come about an hour after I called her and was watching as the debris covering the body was slowly removed. The soil, sand and chalk was brushed carefully away and sealed in bags as though it were an archaeological dig. The matter preserved for later forensic analysis.

The figure beneath slowly came to light, revealing, as I had surmised, the body of a large man, taller than my six foot and broader and thicker-set, wide shoulders. At least, he had been thicker-set. The flesh had withered on his bones. His face had sunk in and his hair was matted and slimy. It was impossible for me to tell his age, but one thing was for certain.

He hadn't been killed by the falling cliff.

He had been in the ground for some time. Again,

I had no way of telling how long he had been there but I hoped that Kate could. The superintendent had wanted me cleared from the site but Kate had insisted that I should stay. So Susan Dean could either wait a few days for the forensic pathologist to come up from Norwich or agree to Kate's wishes and let me observe. It was a small victory, sure enough, but life is often enriched with such little triumphs. I could feel the glare of Superintendent Susan Dean's gaze on me – it was every bit as intense as the bright lights illuminating the dead body, and it warmed me just as much as the jacket that Henry Hill had lent me.

Kate had bent over again, with a scalpel in her hand.

'What are you doing?' asked the super.

'I am going to cut the gloves away.'

'Maybe leave that until we can get the body to a proper forensic table,' suggested Superintendent Dean.

Kate nodded. 'Might be best. I don't know how stable the body will be when we attempt to move him. I'd rather have him as intact as possible to record the evidence.'

'How old was he at the time of death, would you think?'

'Can't say at this stage. Maybe in the range of thirty to fifty.'

'That's quite a big range.'

'When we get him on the table we can do a more detailed analysis, I am just making suppositions here. Which is never wise.'

'Gives us something to check against the missing-persons register,' I said.

'True.'

'How long do you think he has been in the ground, Doctor Walker?'

'I'd say anything up to thirty years, maybe longer.'

'Definitely not recent, then?'

'Not judging by the decomposition. Again, it is hard to tell – the soil conditions play a large part. This is very salty material here.'

'Meaning?' asked Susan Deans.

'Meaning salt is a preservative,' I interjected. Behind her Sergeant Coker suppressed a smile as she swivelled her head to glare at me once more.

'It's Doctor Walker's analysis I want to hear, Delaney.'

'Inspector Delaney is an extremely experienced and senior Metropolitan Police detective, superintendent,' said Kate, a quiet anger gleaming in her eyes. 'Why don't you climb off your high horse and accept help when it is willingly offered?'

'I—'

The superintendent didn't get to finish her sentence as Kate carried on. 'As Jack rightly said, the very high level of salt acts as a preservative in the soil, so I will need some forensic analysis before I can give you any rough approximation of when he was buried.'

Without waiting for a reply, Kate carefully used her hands with painstaking gentleness, moving them over the dead man's body. She peered down to look at his right wrist and then moved closer, gently lifting the sleeve back a little. There was a glint of metal.

'Something?' asked the super.

Kate used a pen to hook the item. 'A wristwatch. Not an expensive one.'

The watch slid down the corpse's wrist and rested against the hand. 'There is a silver inset on the leather strap. With writing on it, but I can't quite make it out.' She lifted her hands away and signalled for the photographer to take shots. 'I can tell you three things for now, though.'

'Go on,' prompted Susan Dean.

'He was not married. At least, he is not wearing a wedding band as far as I can tell. When we get the gloves off we can see if one has been removed – there will be marks, probably.'

'And the other things?'

'He was probably not a manual worker.'

'I gathered that from the suit he was wearing.'

'People wear suits for all kinds of reason, Susan,' I said. 'Weddings, funerals . . . court appearances.'

The superintendent nodded. 'True.'

Hell. Maybe I was making progress with the woman. Was always only a matter of time. The Delaney charm: like I say, they should put it in a bottle.

'Mostly they wear them for work, though, inspector,' she added. 'And, looking at the fraying around the cuffs and lapels, I would say this wasn't an occasional suit.'

Kate opened the jacket out. There was a tailor's label on the inside pocket on the right-hand side. The writing was illegible. 'It's a classic-cut design,' she said. 'And tailored. So he was probably a professional man. To have a suit tailored isn't cheap. But the watch doesn't look like an expensive one.'

'So we have a professional man, somewhere between thirty or fifty—'

'Possibly,' interjected Kate.

'OK, *possibly* between thirty and fifty. And he could have been in the ground for, what, anywhere from a few months to thirty years?'

'Could be longer than that. We won't know until I get the body to the mortuary in Norwich,' said Kate, watching as the forensic photographers took more shots and video footage.

'Better make it quick,' I said as a corner of the marquee came loose, flapping in the wind and letting a spray of freezing rain in. A few uniforms hurried to secure the breach and Kate beckoned to a couple of scene-of-crime officers who came forward with a stretcher.

'And what was the third thing you can tell us?'

'His bones have been broken in several places.'

'As a result of the landslide.'

'It's possible. He is close to the cliff edge, or what is now the cliff edge. Most of the debris has fallen beyond him to form the mound outside this marquee.'

'So what does that tell us?'

'I have no idea. Just telling you what I can deduce at this stage. I wouldn't like to speculate on probable causes. Like I say, when I have him on the table . . .'

'You'll be able to tell if the broken bones are post-mortem or pre-mortem?'

'Yes, I will,' said Kate, watching as the man was delicately manoeuvred onto the stretcher and covered with a waterproof cloth.

'Why the hell would someone bury a person at the base of a cliff?' I asked.

If there was an answer in the howling wind and pelting rain it was in a language I didn't understand.

17

Lunchtime.

I was sitting at the bar again, in my usual corner, watching as the rain poured down the steamed-up windows, blurring the view outside into an Impressionist painting. I could just about make out the hazy shapes of people dashing along the street, seeking cover in shops or rushing to get back to their cars.

I was drinking a cup of coffee out of a glass cup. The coffee came from an expensive machine that the landlord seemed extremely pleased with. I didn't much care for the cup or for the coffee that was in it. It wasn't as strong as I like it but it was hot, though, and that was the main thing. I'd had enough luke-warm coffee to last me a good while. Times past I'd have slipped a shot or two of brandy in it, warm the inner man. But, like I say, those times were past. At least, I hoped they were. It was just good to be in from the weather. It had by no means been a good start to the day but the heat was working its way back into my bones.

There were a few people in the lounge bar for lunch, but not many. The open log fire that was roaring and crackling away was very welcoming but the town was quiet. Unusually quiet for Sheringham, even out of season. If people didn't have to venture out of home or office I quite frankly didn't blame them. Not that there were many offices or office workers in the town. The population of six thousand or so was mainly made up of an older demographic. A lot of retirees. Mind you people did live in the town year round, unlike other places further west – like Blakeney, for example – where most of the property was owned by rich people from London. Bankers and the like who kept a place as an occasional weekend bolt-hole, somewhere they could moor their yacht and chill their champagne. Sheringham might have been a bit of a bucket-and-spade seaside town, but it was a vibrant one with a strong sense of community. It was lived in.

The door to the lounge bar opened and a couple sitting at the window scowled across as the wind blew a light spray of rain in from the street and in their direction. I'm not quite sure what they expected – did they reckon that people should just not walk through the door and go the long way round the pub to come in by the back entrance?

The umbrella that had entered was lowered, revealing its owner: Amy Leigh. She was dressed more soberly than when I'd last seen her, in a matching black skirt and jacket and a smart blouse. Her hair was windswept yet somehow managed to look chic rather than bedraggled. If I hadn't known her I would have had her down as a 'Blakeneyite' type. What we used to call a Sloane Ranger back in the day. But I did know her, and she certainly wasn't that. She rattled her umbrella, oblivious to the scowls she was receiving from the couple at the window table, propped it against the bar and nodded to me. The man by the window made a big show of rattling the business section of the *Daily Telegraph* and the woman made a clearly audible tutting sound. I looked at them steadily and after a moment they suddenly took a much keener interest in their own affairs. Very wise.

Amy pulled up a stool and sat next to me, gesturing at my coffee glass.

'Fancy something stronger?'

I shook my head as a tall young girl with red-streaked blonde hair and who weighed about seven stone came out into the bar, holding a plate in her hand. 'Fifty-eight,' she shouted out, a tad louder than was necessary considering how many people were in the bar.

'Bingo,' I said and smiled.

'Oh, it's you, Delaney,' she said and handed me the plate. 'Your salad sandwich.'

Amy Leigh cocked an eyebrow at me.

'I know, Kate's idea! She thinks I need to lose a few pounds before the wedding. Got me on the Hay Diet.'

'Which would be?'

'No proteins with starch-based foods, and vice versa.'

'In English?'

'You can't have potatoes or bread or pasta with meats and eggs and cheeses and fish, et cetera.'

'You becoming a new man, Jack?'

'Becoming an old man. I am seriously thinking of

buying one of those fisherman's sweaters, whatever they are called.'

'A Jersey or a Guernsey, I believe.'

'Yeah, one of those.' I leaned over and tapped a bell that hung in the corner with my pen, as there didn't seem to be any signs of life behind the bar and Amy looked ready for a drink.

'I'll have a large soda and lime, please,' Amy said to the bespectacled youth who had appeared behind the bar and who looked all of sixteen. I was forty-three now – maybe I was getting old.

'Stick it on my tab, Billy,' I said. I took a bite of my sandwich and registered my displeasure. 'Not even any mayonnaise.'

Amy laughed. 'Salad sandwiches and fisherman's jumpers. You *are* getting old, Delaney,' she said.

'I have to tell you I was out on the Sheringham cliffs at six o'clock this morning, and there were brass monkeys running around desperate to find a welder.'

'I heard about that. They found a dead body.'

'Yes. Know of any large men gone missing from the area over the last thirty years or thereabouts?'

'Well, no. Not really, not off the top of my head, Jack. What about the police – don't they have a missing-persons register?'

'They do and they'll be checking it. Unlikely they will update me on any progress, though.'

'Oh?'

'Superintendent Susan Dean doesn't have me at the top of her favourite-people list.'

'Nor me.'

'Why not?'

'I do a lot of pro-bono work. And legal aid – represent people who can't afford private counsel. If I didn't get some of the people off who she has put through the system, even before the CPS are involved . . .' She shrugged and took a sip of her drink. 'Then maybe her crime-solving figures and statistics would be higher. She's a very political kind of policewoman.'

'I know the sort.'

'And she knows your sort, Delaney. Maybe that's why she hasn't warmed to you.'

'And what sort is that?'

'The sort who is more interested in "nicking wrong un's" than he is in collecting badges.' Her Ray Winstone impersonation was about as convincing as if I had attempted to do Katherine Hepburn. I smiled anyway.

'Maybe I am too lazy, and too old, and too opposed to paperwork to be a political animal.'

'Yeah, and maybe you just like kicking doors in and busting heads.'

'If it gets the job done.'

Amy laughed again. 'You don't fool me, Jack. You do well in your job because you are a lot smarter than you like to let people think you are.'

'You'll have to write that down and I'll see if I can work out what it means later.'

'I'll speak to my uncle,' she said, ignoring me. 'He may know of some missing people from that time.'

'I'd be grateful.'

'Why the interest?'

'I think the guy was murdered and he was found on property that I am a security consultant for.'

'Not at the time he was murdered, you weren't. If he was murdered at all, that is. Is there any word on the autopsy?'

'Not yet – the body has been taken to the morgue at Kelling Hospital. Didn't want to risk transporting it too far, given its condition. And Kate is waiting to be given the go-ahead to do the preliminary work.'

Amy looked surprised. 'Kate's going to be doing it?'

'Probably. Seems Norwich is a bit tied up for a day or so.'

'He's waited this long.' She took another sip of her drink. 'Shouldn't think a couple of days' or so wait more will matter in the grand scheme of things.'

'Probably not, but I get the sense that Superintendent Susan Dean wants to steal a march. Bust the case, as it were, before more dazzling urbanites from the city come up and steal her thunder.'

She looked at me critically. 'And is that perhaps why you are taking so keen an interest? Looking mayhap to steal her thunder with your own dazzling big-city skills.'

I looked back at her impassively. 'I just like to solve a mystery.'

'Sure you do. Anyway, I hoped to catch you here, and the mobile-phone signal is down . . . again.'

'I know.'

'I understand you spoke to Helen yesterday and had a word with her builders?'

'That I did.'

'It seems to have worked.'

'What do you mean?' I asked, a little surprised.

'She phoned me late this morning. On the landline, obviously! Said she'd come to an arrangement with the builders and they were going to finish the job for a lot less than they had said before.'

'Which builders?'

'The original ones. You obviously got your message across.'

'I kicked his ladder away and punched his mate a few times about as hard as I could. Don't think I made much of a dent in either one's confidence.'

Amy looked at me, puzzled. I outlined to her how the meeting had gone down and filled her in on Superintendent Susan Dean's take on the situation.

'They've made an official complaint?'

'No. Not quite. But she made it clear that she would throw the book at me if I hassled them any more.'

'Nice.' The young solicitor compressed her lips in distaste.

'I might have flashed a warrant card and implied I was on the job around here, mind you,' I offered by way of explanation for the super's irritation.

'So why the volte-face, then? Why would they backtrack on what they said?'

'How did Helen Middleton sound to you?'

Amy Leigh considered it for a minute. 'On reflection, not as happy as she should have done. She did say to thank you for what you'd done, but not to proceed with any further actions. She was happy to proceed under the new terms.'

'But she didn't sound it?'

'No. Now I come to think of it she didn't seem particularly buoyed.'

I nodded.

'What do you think?'

'I think the boys have paid her a visit. Obviously Superintendent Dean has given them the impression that my hands are tied.'

'Aren't they? Given what the police have said?'

'Just think of me as Harry Houdini,' I said and pushed the half-eaten sandwich away.

'What are you going to do?'

'What I said I would do.'

'Which is?'

'Help Helen Middleton, and frighten the boys some more.'

'And how are you going to do that?

I looked at Amy steadily. 'Do you really want to know?'

She considered for a moment or two and then smiled a kind of grimace. 'I guess I probably don't.'

'Good guess.'

'I don't want you getting into trouble over this, Jack. I asked you as a favour.'

'Trouble is what I do, Amy.'

She looked at me for another long moment and then laughed. 'You crack me up, Delaney.'

I gestured to the barmaid. 'Order me up a bacon sandwich and get me a pint of Guinness, would you, darlin'? And get this young woman a proper drink.'

18

I looked up at the sky. It was clear now, apart from a few long, crimson streaks of cloud. The first time for a long while. There was a freshening wind coming from the sea but nothing like the earlier storms. Maybe they had blown themselves out. The town smelled fresh and clean, and the ozone was almost as invigorating as the Guinness I had just drunk.

I walked up to my car which was parked by The Crown pub on the seafront. A bunch of seagulls were sitting on the promenade wall, eyeing me suspiciously. The seagulls didn't like it out of season – there were no unwary tourists to pinch chips from.

I climbed into my old Saab and after about the third attempt to start it the engine kicked into life. I pulled out and was about to head up Gun Street and pay a visit to Helen Middleton when Sergeant Coker stepped out in the road and held up his hand in a 'Halt, who goes there?' gesture.

I wound down the window and looked across as he leaned in.

'Your wife told me I might find you at the Lobby. I guess I just missed you.'

'What's happening?'

'She's got the go-ahead to proceed with the post-mortem. Thought you might like to come with me.'

'Does Super Susan know about this?'

'She knows about the autopsy.'

'But not about me attending?'

'No.'

'You think she's going to like that?'

'Does this face look bothered?'

I looked at his healthy, ruddy complexion and the amusement in his eyes.

'I'll see you there,' I said.

Kelling Heath Hospital is an old building a few miles from Holt. As you swing down the switchback road from Bodham to Upper Kelling you have to slow down to thirty miles an hour. Not that everyone did. As I said, the normal rules of the Queen's Highway didn't seem to apply hereabouts. Maybe something to do with Boadicea. I pulled across the road and turned right and then right again, drove up and managed to find a parking spot in front of the building.

A young nurse told me where to go as I explained why I was there. I thanked him and walked through a couple of corridors down to the old morgue. Kelling Heath Hospital is now a rehabilitation unit for convalescing patients in the main. But it had been a TB sanatorium in the past and therefore housed a small morgue.

I pushed the door open and walked in. Sergeant Coker had beaten me there but, as I had had to stop to refuel the car at the garage on the coast road, I didn't hold it against him.

Kate was gloved, gowned and masked and a younger woman similarly garbed was standing beside her. A forensic photographer who I recognised from the crime scene on the beach earlier was standing by, ready to record the process, and a forensic assistant was gowned and gloved like Kate and ready to help her.

Neither the sergeant nor I had bothered to gown and mask up. We stood by the door, watching. I hate post-mortems but this was by no means the worst that I had attended. Because the body had been partly mummified in the salty ground there weren't the usual aromas that went with the procedure. Kate had once told me that smell was particulate and explained what it meant, and I didn't feel any happier for having the knowledge of it.

'Just about to begin, Jack,' she said as I closed the door behind me.

'You were never here,' said the sergeant in a stage whisper to me.

'Certainly not.'

Kate began by removing the cadaver's gloves, revealing large hands, the flesh on them pale and withered, the bones prominent beneath it. As Kate had surmised there was no band on the man's wedding finger.

'There is no sign that he has ever had a wedding ring,' Kate said, talking towards a microphone that was recording the progress of the post-mortem.

'So a single man in his late twenties or thirties who has never married,' I speculated out loud, but quietly, to the red-haired man beside me.

'Gay?' said the sergeant.

'Who knows?' I shrugged.

'I am now spraying some alcohol spirit on the white-metal inset on his watch strap,' said Kate, and proceeded to do as she said. Then, very delicately, she swabbed the metal with what looked like a Q-tip to me but probably had some specialist technical pathology name.

'Looks to me like the inscription reads: 'Amor Vincit Omnia.'

'What's that supposed to mean?' the ruddy-faced sergeant asked Kate.

'It's Latin,' I answered for her. 'Love conquers all.'

'Definitely gay, then,' said Coker.

He would have laughed but Kate shot him a look that made him think better of it.

It took Kate and her assistant a while to carefully cut off the clothes that the dead man had been wearing. They were bagged and logged. Naked he was pale-skinned and the flesh of his torso was every bit as deteriorated as that of his hands had been. It was as though the skin had simply been stretched over his skeleton. He had a thin, flat wooden crucifix on a chain around his neck. Kate looked closely at the damaged bones, snicked the chain on the crucifix and handed it to a forensics officer for bagging. Then she turned to us.

'I can't tell you if these broken bones were pre- or

post-mortem. But I can tell you this man was murdered.'

'How so?'

'He was stabbed, middle of his chest. Right in the heart.'

'Can you put a date on when it happened?' asked the sergeant.

'Not yet. The soil conditions where he was buried make it very hard to be even approximately accurate. We'll need lab analysis. And that will take time.'

'I guess we need to find out who he is,' I said.

'Good place to start,' Kate agreed and turned back to the body on the examination table. 'John Doe needs a name.'

19

It was late by the time I got back onto the coast road and headed west out of Sheringham once more.

It hadn't rained since the late morning, which was some good news for that day at least. I had stayed with the sergeant and watched the rest of the post-mortem. Saw the dead man disassembled bit by bit. What was left of his organs weighed and recorded. His stomach opened. Its contents removed for further analysis.

I regretted breaking my diet and having that bacon sandwich.

I had wound down the window for a minute or so to let the cold air blow over me as I headed for the coast road. But it hadn't made me feel any better so I had wound it up again and cranked up the heater. The sun was dipping ahead of me nearly into the ocean again, and although it wasn't raining it was still cold. Bloody cold.

I looked at the sky that was purpling and darkening now, and figured we would have a frost again tonight.

I drove into Helen Middleton's garden, the three-quarter shingle crunching satisfyingly beneath my wheels. I zipped my jacket up to the top and leaned on the doorbell. I hadn't phoned her. The lights were on in her bungalow and I could hear classical music playing, but my spider senses were tingling. Something wasn't right here.

I leaned on the bell once more and was relieved when I heard the sound of the music being lowered. A few moments later the door opened. But it only opened a few inches. A chain had been fitted to the inside.

Helen Middleton peered out. 'Oh, it's you, Jack. Can I help you with something?'

'I just wanted to have a quick word, Helen,' I said, smiling reassuringly.

'I am a little bit busy,'

'It won't take a minute.'

She hesitated and then closed the door. It opened again a moment later.

'I see you've had a chain fitted.'

'Well, you can't be too careful, can you?'

'I guess not.'

I didn't think it would be fair to point out that a small security chain like that had no chance of stopping either Bill Collier or his associate if they wanted to get into her house. Wasn't entirely sure what would, short of a fortified steel door.

I followed Helen into her living room. As neat as ever. The figurines gleaming, the surfaces shiny, a faint hint of polish in the air.

'I was about to pour myself a small sherry. Can I get you one?' she asked me.

Not my nip of choice but I nodded. 'Thank you. That would be very nice.'

'What part of Ireland are you from?' she asked as she walked to a cabinet and poured out two measures of sherry into a couple of matching glasses.

'Cork.'

'Cork City?'

'Near it. Ballydehob.'

'I've never been.'

'Most people have never been to Ballydehob.'

'I meant to Ireland.'

Helen's hand had been shaking as she poured the drinks, the neck of the bottle rattling against the rims of the glasses. It wasn't me she was nervous of. I took a sip of the sherry, which was surprisingly dry. Probably a good one but I had no real framework of reference.

I looked around the room. There was no sign of the dog. The music playing was calming, soothing.

'Where's Bruno?' I asked.

She flinched a little. 'In my bedroom. Having a nap.'

Bruno started barking. 'Sounds like he might have woken up,' I said and produced a soft dog toy in the shape of a blue octopus from my pocket. 'I brought him a little present.'

'That's kind of you. Hang on, I'll fetch him.'

There was moisture in her eyes as she left hurriedly and I heard her put the chain back on the front door. I guess I could tell what the Brothers Grim had threatened Helen Middleton with and I didn't find my dislike of them lessening any.

She came back, holding the dog in her arms, and looked at me for a moment or two before speaking.

'I don't want you doing anything that will bring harm to him.'

'I won't do that, I promise,' I said.

'I am an old lady. He is the only thing that I have left. Apart from my house and my work.'

'I understand, Helen. The innocent have the right not to be afraid, especially in their own homes.'

'I can't help being afraid. But they should not be allowed to get away with this. I realise that now.'

'I took the wrong approach with them. I thought the threat of the law would be enough. But I of all people should know that sometimes it isn't.'

'I don't wish you to be getting into any further trouble. I understand the police have reprimanded you.'

'I can take care of myself.'

Helen nodded thoughtfully. 'I think you can.'

'You just take care of Bruno,' I said and handed him the toy. He held it between his teeth and it set his tail whipping again.

'Thank you, Jack,' she said.

'It's just a little toy,' I replied. 'It didn't cost much.'

'I wasn't talking about the toy.'

'I know.'

20

Our house was built in the mid-nineteenth century.

A fisherman's cottage in brick and flint. There was a small front garden, with steps leading up to the front door bisecting it. Shingled areas on both sides, with plants and seaside ephemera: a few lobster pots, a small anchor, an olive tree that Kate's cousin had planted in a large half-barrel. Coastal kitsch. But it worked and it was a million miles from my old place in Kentish Town.

I was standing in the farmhouse-style kitchen, looking out onto the pergola and the patio that stretched down to the garden proper. It was half-covered and in the summer and early autumn I had barbecued there while Kate cradled our baby Jade and sat with Siobhan on a bench and watched me. Looking out at the darkness now it seemed a long time ago. But the night was filled with stars. One of the best things about being away from the city was the night sky. You could actually see the stars when the sky was clear. Millions of them.

'Penny for them?' Kate asked.

'I'll give you a kiss instead,' I said and made good on my promise.

'Nice.'

'I know.'

'What are you going to do about Helen Middleton?'

'Probably best you don't know.'

'I'm going up to bed to read,' she said and kissed me again. 'And Siobhan said to remind you that you promised to read her a story, or make one up like you usually do.'

'OK.'

'And please, Jack. Nothing about drugs or dead hookers or violent crime.'

'OK.'

'I mean it. You haven't had her English teacher asking me where she gets some of the stories from when she has to write a holiday essay. Her "What I did last summer" piece nearly had them calling social services.'

Kate went through the door that led from the kitchen to a narrow, steep, typically Norfolk stairway. I waited for a few moments, heard her talking to Siobhan and then pulled out my mobile phone and punched the button on a speed-dial contact.

'Is that yourself, Jack?'

I smiled. The familiar voice bringing memories flooding back.

I was nine years old and walking back from school alone. My best friend Rory had been off sick with measles and I was forbidden to visit him. That suited me just fine. I had seen kids with the measles right enough and could do without them myself, thank you very much. I'd catch up with Rory when he was well and uncontaged, or whatever it was they called it. Like me, my mate Rory was big for his age. Everyone said when he grew up he'd either be a policeman or a professional wrestler. It was their joke. What Rory wanted to do when he grew up was be a carpenter like his da. Heck, his ma always joked, sure enough he could just pick the trees out of the ground, he'd have no need for lumberjacks and saws for his raw materials. Rory took it in good humour, he knew his da bought his wood from the trade store in Bantry mainly, but he humoured his mother. You had to keep the women on your side.

Even at that age I agreed with him on that one. I didn't know what I wanted to do when I grew up, though. They talked about it often enough but I couldn't fix myself on anything. Plenty of time for that. Fireman one week. A soldier a few years back before the Troubles flared up in earnest again. Secretly I sometimes dreamed of being a priest. I could see myself standing up there in the pulpit, holding everybody in awe as I railed and castigated. I was not so hot at the academicals, however, as I called them back then and I minded how the black crows and the penguins knew everything about everything, and that must take a powerful lot of book studying.

I bent down to pick up a pebble form the path. Feck it, I thought, I'm only nine years old – I have my whole life ahead of me. I threw the stone, arcing it high in the air to clatter down on the salt-crusted rocks on the beach below, when I heard the cry. And I recognised the voice.

I rushed down the path and around the corner. And there, sure enough, was Liam Corrigan, my cousin. Liam was a couple of years younger than me, a few inches shorter, and was surrounded by four older boys with mischief on their faces and sticks in their hands. I could see that Liam had tears in his eyes, that he was trying to hold back, and a small trickle of blood was running down from his nose.

I knew the other boys, sure enough. All Linehans. All trouble. Like the family had always been.

'Brave of you to be taking on the one boy,' I said to the eldest of them.

Gerry Linehan looked at me and grinned, strolling over. 'You want to join in, do you? Do you want some of—'

But he never finished the sentence as I smashed my fist furiously and suddenly into his nose. The boy dropped, squealing, to his knees. I snatched up the stick from his hand and turned to the three remaining Linehans.

'Come on, then, ya gobshites.'

I waved the stick in front of me and pushed Liam towards the road. 'Get out of here.'

And as Liam ran off up the road for help, I turned and faced the others, a fury in me as they circled me as warily as a pack of dogs would approach a wounded wolf.

Had help not arrived when it did, things might have gone a lot worse for me. But, as it was, that was the first time I ended up in hospital for Liam. On that occasion it was for a fractured wrist. On the second occasion it was for something far more serious.

'He's coming round.'

I heard the voice and tried to open my eyes. Christ, I felt awful. As if I had been run over by a herd of cattle. Every muscle in my body ached. But most of all there was a stabbing pain in my side, and I remembered where I was and why.

'God bless you, Jack. You've done a marvellous thing.'

I blinked my eyes and could just about make out my aunt looking down, smiling gratefully, and my mother, beautiful as she always was, with hair like Maureen O'Sullivan's and every bit as pretty, as my da always said.

'Is he going to be all right?' I asked.

'Yes, Jack,' ma said, taking my hand and patting it. He's going to be just grand. You both are.'

The fact that she crossed herself immediately after saying it might have given others cause for concern, but I was sixteen years old now and invincible.

'You've saved his life, Jack. You've saved his life,' cried his aunt effusively, bursting into tears.

I shrugged. 'Sure, it was only a kidney.'

I smiled at the memory. And then the smile faded as I remembered how my cousin had repaid me. Many years later in the lock-up of a murdering gangster called Mickey Ryan in London.

There was a metallic clang. I looked across to see the gorilla of a henchman putting a toolbox on the workbench that ran along the whole left-hand side of the garage.

'You might wonder why you are still alive, Delaney.'

'Must be my guardian angel.'

Ryan laughed. His blue eyes sparkling with amusement. 'I wonder if you'll still be laughing when my man here goes to work on you with a pair of needle-tooth pliers.'

Liam stepped forward. 'Nobody said anything about that.'

'Nobody points a gun at me and gets away with it. You're going to learn that, Delaney. And that grassing tub of lard Norrell is going to be next.' He turned to Liam. 'Put one in his gut, give him something to think about.'

Liam raised the pistol he had been holding in his right hand: a semi-automatic with a silencer. I could see no mercy, no compassion in his eyes as he pulled the trigger.

The minder made a sound like a dog swallowing a fly and dropped to the floor, a hand fluttering towards his heart but not making it. Liam pointed the gun at Mickey Ryan.

'The fuck you think you're doing?'

'The fuck you think I'm doing?'

Ryan shook his head. 'We had a deal.'

'I don't make deals with scum. Gut shot, wasn't it?' He pulled the trigger again, and Mickey Ryan

dropped to his knees, squealing and holding his stomach. 'Hurts, doesn't it?'

Ryan's face had gone purple and he hissed between his teeth. But if they were words he was trying to speak they were not intelligible to the human ear.

Liam grabbed a Stanley knife from the toolbox and slashed the ropes binding my arms.

He smiled. 'I made some calls after you left. Figured out what was going on and realised you'd be way out of your depth.'

'I had it covered.'

'Sure you did, cousin. But you weren't going to kill him, were you?'

I didn't answer.

'Which means that one way or another he would have ended up killing you.'

'Maybe.'

'No "maybe" about it.'

'What did you have to hit me for, then?'

'You might be ten kinds of death wish walking on legs, Jack. But I still enjoy my life. I did what I had to do. And you should be grateful, so take a Panadol and shut the fuck up with the whining already.'

Ryan gurgled again, hissing through wet lips, his face contorted with pain. 'Listen . . .'

Liam turned to me and held the gun out. 'Do you want to do it?'

I made no move to take the pistol. Liam nodded, then fired two bullets one after the other into the kneeling man's head. Ryan slumped sideways and the gurgling stopped.

I looked at the dead body. Not sure what to think any more. 'What now?'

'Now, cousin, we walk away from here.'

'We can't. There's DNA all over the place. You go. Leave me the gun.'

Liam reached into his overcoat and pulled out a large brown packet. 'Did you know Mickey Ryan was in big with the old IRA? Back in the 1970s?'

'No.'

Liam nodded. 'Back in the day he made a fair few bob out of it. Pissed a fair few people off, too. People who didn't take the laying down of arms at all happily. Formed new groups.'

'The Real IRA.'

Liam shrugged. 'Amongst others. Either way. He's on a list. And this . . .' he tossed the packet onto the workbench '. . . is the boys' old friend.'

'Semtex?'

'There won't be enough left of Mickey Ryan, his sidekick, or this garage to fill a teaspoon, let alone any trace of our DNA.'

I nodded. Micky Ryan was the man who had been responsible for my wife's death when she'd been torn apart by a shotgun blast in a Pinner petrol station. I looked down at his dead body. It didn't feel like closure.

I just felt empty.

'I guess that makes us even, Liam.'

I snapped back into the present and took a deep breath as the phone was answered. 'Liam,' I said. 'I need a favour again.'

'Anytime, Jack. You know that.'

'Our slate's clean.'

'Never going to happen, cousin. We look out for each other. What do you need?'

'I need someone dealing with.'

21

I stood in the doorway and looked at my sleeping wife-to-be.

Her book, Hilary Mantel's *Wolf Hall*, had fallen from her hand and lay face down beside her on the bed. Kate preferred her violence, crimes and murder in the distant past; preferably Tudor, for some reason. But she had been reading this particular book for a while and hadn't made much progress into it. She'd probably read about half a page before nodding off. Having a young baby to look after meant that she grabbed her opportunities to sleep whenever she could, it wasn't a literary criticism on her part.

It had been a long day for both of us, and I knew that going back to forensic pathology on this case today had taken its toll on her. She had given up that particular job for a reason. At the time she had decided to quit she was pregnant, and neither she nor I were aware of it. She had been sick one morning after being called to the scene of a particularly gruesome murder and decided that she couldn't do it any more. It had been morning sickness but she knew it was more than that in hindsight. I looked across at our baby daughter, Jade, who was named after Kate's mother. She too was sleeping peacefully, her eyes closed but a smile still playing on her lips. I couldn't blame Kate for wanting to give up that aspect of her job. Or for giving up on London and bringing both the girls to a safer part of the world. I guessed she had gone into pathology because it meant she didn't have to get emotionally involved, a way of dealing with the demons of her past that had haunted her, had fractured her in her soul or psyche or spirit or whatever you want to call it. I had attempted to drown my feelings in the comfort of alcohol after my wife's death, and Kate had to keep those childhood demons at bay by working among the dead. The living needed more from her than she was able to give at that time. Kate had saved me, our daughter had saved her. Maybe I played a part, I don't know. One thing I did know was that I was going to keep her safe, keep them all safe, whatever it took.

22

I tapped on the door across the corridor and my daughter Siobhan called me in.

She too was reading. Sitting up in bed with a copy of Arthur Ransome's *Coot Club*, which involved two friends of the *Swallows and Amazons* children having more water-based adventures on the Norfolk Broads, apparently. She had been given it to read by her English teacher who was no doubt keen to show her a pleasanter way of life than the gritty reality of the great Metropolis that we had left behind and which had evidently crept into some of Siobhan's creative endeavours. Personally, I wasn't worried and Kate agreed with me that there was a certain cathartic healing in writing out the stuff of her nightmares. Kate herself knew only too well the side effects of bottling up childhood trauma. The brain can apply a particularly potent pressure. But there is a yin and a yang to everything and, if Siobhan took comfort from escaping to the middle-class fantasy world of high jinks on the jolly old Broads in 1934, then that was fine by me too.

'How's the book?' I asked.

'Can we get a sailing boat?' she replied.

There's a downside to everything, too.

'Maybe in the spring, when the weather is better, we can hire a boat from Wroxham and take a trip, see how you like it in real life.'

'Got to be a sailboat, though. Motorboats are for foreigners and hullabaloos.'

'I see.'

'Foreigners are holidaymakers. It's not racist.'

'That's good to know.'

'Not proper Norfolk people like us.'

I sat on the bed beside her. 'We're proper Norfolk people now, are we?'

'We can be if we want to be.'

I nodded reassuringly. Sometimes things are simpler when you are eight years old. But, then again, maybe she was right. We are all made in God's image, apparently. But what we make of ourselves, after that, is largely down to us. I hadn't made such a good job of it lately; maybe I should listen to my daughter more. From the mouths of babes.

'Tell me a story, then,' she commanded, settling herself back on the pillow.

'OK – do you want to hear the tale of Black Shuck?' I asked, mindful of Kate's instructions.

'Black Shuck. What is that?'

'It's a local tale.'

'A Norfolk tale.'

'Better than that: a North Norfolk tale from this very coast.'

Siobhan made saucers of her eyes, a tad over-dramatically perhaps. But she was a Delaney, after all.

'Go on, then,' she said.

'So now, twelve hundred years or so ago on the North Norfolk coast early in the month of July when the sun was a blazing star in the midday sky and the corn was golden and tall and ready for harvest. All the talk in the village of Sheringham was about the carnival that was coming up in the following month. A committee of the village elders, the local druid and a strange woman who lived in a cave gathered to prepare for it. It was a time of feasting and laughter, of wine and song. There would be displays of strength and racing, and each year a carnival queen was to be appointed. And that year they chose a fair maiden by the name of Eadlin, which actually means princess in the Anglo-Saxon tongue so maybe her parents knew she would be crowned a princess. Even if it was only for the week of the Sheringham carnival. Everybody called her Eadie and everybody loved her.'

'Was she pretty?'

'She was fifteen years old and the one man who loved her most was Owen Tregatthen, the druid. And he had pledged her parents the princely sum of three goats if they would give her hand in marriage to him.'

'Wasn't she too young to be married?'

'Not in Norfolk at that time. Now, the town had been raided for many years by the Viking warriors from across the North Sea. And that year the elders had decided that they had had enough. A sacrifice had to be made to the sea gods. The committee elected to take the carnival queen to the top of the Beeston

Bump. And as the sun set into the sea at the end of the summer solstice they were to bind her to a stake in the middle of a large bonfire that they had built and then sacrifice her.

'The solstice arrived and the sunset approached. The villagers took the young maiden Eadlin and led her up the hill to the summit of the Beeston Bump. Approaching on the sea as the sun set, the flames of a torch could be seen as the Viking craft drew near to the shore. It was a long wooden boat and at the helm there was a dragon's head, with blazing eyes painted red.

'The villagers cast their own burning brands into the bonfire that they had built, and the flames crackled and flared upward, dancing in the cool evening breeze. The crowd fell to their knees and prayed to the god of the seas.

'A tempest arose, the like of which had never been seen before. So that the Viking craft carrying the men who had come to take their loot was hurled beneath the waves and the men drowned. But just as quickly as the storm had come it vanished, when the sea god realised that the druid had tricked him. Had tricked all the villagers, too, because the figure tied to the stake was not a real person at all but an effigy with a waxen face and a wig.'

'Like our own Guy Fawkes?'

'Exactly so, darling. It was too late to bring back the drowned Viking warriors but the sea god looked down and saw that the sole survivor of the shipwrecked vessel was a black dog. Paddling in the now-calm waters.

And the sea god took his vengeance, for when that dog reached the shore he had become the size of a small horse, with wild shaggy hair and huge saucer-like eyes that flashed with fire.'

'Black Shuck!'

'Black Shuck indeed. And since that fearful day over twelve hundred years ago, when the sun sets over Sheringham and Overstrand, then Black Shuck comes out to prowl, loping and hunting, along river bed and shoreline, on the clifftops or up in the dark pine woods, along the quiet country lanes, leaping over flint walls in churchyards and cemeteries. Jumping out, headless sometimes, from behind old gravestones, seeking retribution on the druid who had tried to cheat the gods. And if anyone hears him behind them, howling like a very banshee from Cork, then they'd best make sure not to set their eyes upon his fearsome form. For if they do, they will be dead within the year.'

'Yes, but that's just a story, isn't it?' my daughter asked, clutching the bed sheet up to her chin.

I leaned over and kissed her on the forehead. 'Course it is, darling. You're safe up here.'

23

The four men stood in the dark. All in dark clothing, all with balaclavas over their heads under black watch caps.

Two of the men held sawn-off shotguns. The other two held baseball bats. They were motionless. Silent. Their breaths misting in the cold air. They were waiting.

They knew how to wait.

Bill Collier flicked the on switch on the CD player mounted under his dashboard and pressed PLAY.

Dolly Parton started singing 'It's a Hard-Candy Christmas.' Bill didn't care that Christmas was a couple of months away yet. He liked Dolly Parton. He had promised himself that one of these days he would make the pilgrimage to Dollywood, Dolly Parton's huge theme park based in the good old US of A, way down south in Tennessee. A temple to the lady herself. With accommodation and shows and amusement rides. And, as he had often said to his strong but dim associate, he'd sure like to take a ride on Dolly's special attractions. He smiled to himself at the thought, felt himself stiffening as her throaty voice sang about the loneliness of a single woman at the festive season. She wouldn't be alone for long if he had his way. She'd have some hard candy, sure enough. And not the sort you could buy in a sweetshop.

Bill was feeling pretty pleased with himself. He'd had a couple of pints of Kronenbourg in The Ship and a smoke of the good stuff in the pub's car park. He'd booked an Eastern European escort from Cromer, with big blonde hair, artificially augmented breasts and a willingness to take part in certain sexual practices that some of the local girls in Norwich baulked at. She was due to arrive at his house in about an hour and a half and he moved his crotch in time to the country carol in eager anticipation. The speed he had taken and the little blue pill he had dropped in expectation of a good long session probably helped his mood as well.

He drove his car into his driveway as Dolly finished her song, maintaining that she would be fine although she clearly felt she wouldn't be, or at least the character personified in the song wouldn't be. But old Bill, he was going to be fine. Pretty fine and dandy. And that was a fact.

Except it wasn't.

He clicked the locking button on his car key and was walking to the front door of his house when the men in balaclavas stepped out from the darkness.

Part Two

24

Late October, early morning and I was running up a hill wearing thermal underwear, joggers, a couple of shirts, a hoodie and a black watch cap on my head.

It was bitterly cold out, the wind still scalpelling in from the north, but I had worked up a sweat and certainly wasn't feeling the chill. It was a routine I had got into. I got up early with Kate and the girls. We had breakfast. Kate dropped Siobhan off at the local school, and took the baby with her into work. They didn't have a crèche as such, but there was an informal arrangement and if needed we had a nanny we could call upon. I'd come to the office, change into my running outfit and jog over the Beeston Bump, over the railway and up Beacon Hill, the long stretch that climbs to the highest point in Norfolk at a place called Roman Camp.

There has never been any evidence of a Roman presence there, mind: the name was made up by drivers of horse-drawn cabs around the turn of the nineteenth century to make the place sound more exciting to tourists. It certainly seemed to work. Mainly because of the views. It was called Beacon Hill because the area below and to the north of it, The Runtons on the coast, was at one time one of the most dangerous areas on the Norfolk coast for piratical activity and Viking invaders. A beacon lit on the top of that hill, warning of incoming people with hostile intentions, could be seen for miles around. And it is true to say that when the weather permits the views there are spectacular.

It was still a bastard to run up, though. Especially getting towards winter when the narrow paths that thread though the tangled trees growing up the long hill get wet and muddy. The wind had scattered torn branches and dead vegetation everywhere, making the path an obstacle course.

But I had made myself a promise. Four runs a week at least. Maybe when winter bit really deep I would join a gym. But not yet: the spandex and weight machine brigade had never appealed to me.

So despite the cold I was sweating and breathing heavily when I got back to my trailer-van office.

The mobile phone on my desk was trilling and dancing a little as I unlocked the door and entered. I picked it up.

'Delaney,' I said.

'Jesus, Jack! You having a wank or something?'

I recognised the sweet feminine tones of my old boss back in the Met.

'Hi, Diane,' I replied, getting my breath back. I heard an intake of breath – Diane Campbell had scant regard for the law about smoking in public places. I could picture her in my mind's eye standing by her window, puffing smoke and watching the uniforms come and go in the car park below her office.

'So how's the boondocks treating you, Cowboy?'

'Very peaceful. You know, seashores and pine woodlands. Air you can breathe.'

'Sounds like a fucking nightmare to me.'

'Kate likes it.'

'Is the mad woman still going to marry you?'

'Seems like it. We do have a child or two, you know.'

'Quite the nuclear family.'

'Are you going to make it for the big day?'

'Damn right! Promised Kate I'd make sure you wouldn't do a runner.'

'More than my life's worth.'

'She *is* a determined kind of lady.'

'It's Siobhan I'm scared of.'

I could hear Diane laughing on the other end of the phone. I missed that laugh. I missed Sally Cartwright and the others back in the Met. I even missed that miserable old bastard Bob Wilkinson.

'So when are you coming back to the real world, Jack?' she asked as if reading my thoughts. 'There's more important work for you to do down here in the big city than up there at the back of beyond finding sheep rustlers and pig pokers.'

'For a lesbian you're not particularly politically correct, are you, Diane?'

'If it squeals like a pig and wallows in mud. Isn't that what they say? Just telling it like it is.'

'Working on a murder case, actually.'

'Who's the client?'

'No client as such.'

'Assisting the police with their enquiries?'

'Not in an official capacity. The lady sheriff round here doesn't exactly warm to me.'

'Is she a dyke too?'

I laughed this time. 'I have absolutely no idea. She's a ball-buster, sure enough.'

'You've always had big balls, Jack. Tell me about the murder.'

'Body buried near a cliff. Part of the cliff collapses. The body is exposed.'

'How long had she or he been there?'

'A he, and a good few years.'

'So it's a cold case.'

'Pretty cold.'

'We have plenty of live ones down here.'

'As ever was. So why are you calling, Diane?'

'Like I said, we could you use back down here. Christmas is coming, Cowboy. The goose is getting fat and your gap-year vacation is coming to an end.'

'It's a sabbatical.'

'We both know what it is.'

'Sorry, Diane, I'm not cut out for the politics of Paddington Green.'

'Purpose of the call.'

'Meaning?'

'Meaning the plans to merge us into Paddington Green have been shelved. They are focusing on what our American chums call homeland security. White City is going back to being its own centre of excellence in the big fight against crime in our own special part of the naked city.'

'Good for you.'

'And for you, Jack. Like I said, I want you back. Resources are stretched – I need good people. People who I can work with. People who can get the job done. You, in short.'

'I made a commitment to Kate.'

'You made a commitment to take a year out. You're renting a house and it was always on the cards that you would come back – isn't that right?'

'I don't know, Diane. I kinda like it up here.'

'I'll leave you to chew on it, big feller. I know you, is all I'm saying. Give me a call.'

She hung up. I looked at the phone thoughtfully. Damn the woman. She was right.

She did know me.

25

The shower in the caravan was small but it was hot at least.

I had been standing under it for five minutes, letting the water wash over me and chewing over what my old boss – still technically my boss, in fact – had put to me. The New Year was a long way off yet. Plenty of time to make a decision when push came to shove. I was rinsing shampoo out of my hair when I heard two sirens, both of them police. They were coming in my direction. Then, by the sound of it, two squad cars screeched to a halt right outside and the sirens cut off in mid-shriek. So I figured they had come for me.

I figured right. There was a hammering on the door.

'Police! Open up!'

'It's locked – give me a minute,' I called out and turned off the shower. But it seemed that the North Norfolk Constabulary had little patience. I heard a crunch, footsteps and then a familiar voice shouting out.

'Delaney, get out here.' It was Superintendent Susan Dean.

'You want to give me a minute, Susan?'

'No, I don't. Get your arse out here now!'

I shrugged. I of all people knew the authority of the law. I opened the door of the shower cubicle and walked out.

'Do you want to pass me that towel, please?' I asked.

She looked at me for a second, shocked, a flush creeping across her face. Then she turned around. 'Get that clown dressed and down the nick and if he gives you any trouble . . . taser him!' she said to a couple of uniformed male plods and stomped out the door. I picked up the towel and headed to the bedroom. 'Give me five minutes,' I said.

'I'll give you two minutes,' said a broad-shouldered constable in his twenties.

'Or what?'

He didn't seem to have a response to that so I left him to consider his options while I got dressed.

Sheringham police station was built on the site of the new Tesco supermarket.

Tesco had been at war with many of the good people of Sheringham for over fourteen years before they finally got the local council to give them permission to build in the town. Part of the deal was that they had to build a new fire station, community centre and police station. Maybe they had placed the cop shop in their car park because they feared some kind of vandalism reprisals. But in fact the supermarket was pretty well used.

As police stations go it certainly wasn't a Paddington Green. It wasn't a White City. Just a small local police station for local people. It did have a couple of holding cells, though, and I was being marched straight into one. Watched by Susan Dean.

'Why don't you just tell us where you were last night at nine o'clock, Delaney?'

'Like I said, superintendent, I am perfectly happy to make a statement. After I have discussed the matter, as I am entitled under law, with my legal representative.'

'Amy Leigh is on her way, Delaney. Why don't you just stop pissing me off? It won't turn out well for you.'

'Why don't you let me have a word with my client, superintendent?' asked Amy Leigh from the doorway. 'I am sure everything can be cleared up.'

Susan Dean snorted and clacked away on her heels as the uniforms showed Amy into the holding cell and shut the door on us.

'What's going on, Jack?'

I shrugged.

'Bill Collier was found by his colleague this morning. He had been tied up, doused with petrol and told by four masked men who had captured him that they would be back later to set fire to him. They also stole his car.'

I shrugged again. 'Why on Earth should the police think that has anything to do with me?'

'I don't know, Jack. Maybe something to do with you kicking a ladder from under his feet and knocking his mate unconscious.'

'He wasn't unconscious. He was a little dazed, I'll grant you that.'

'And the fact that one of the assailants had an Irish accent.'

I pointed a finger at her. 'That's racist.'

Amy shook her head and sighed. 'You got an alibi?'

'Do I need one?'

'Don't know. Hard to tell what their investigation will throw up. But if you do have one, it might just get you out of here.'

'You can't say you are unhappy about what happened to Collier. He threatened to kill Helen Middleton's dog.'

Amy held a hand up. 'Just stop there, Jack. I know I told you to frighten him. But I was talking in a metaphorical way.'

'People like Bill Collier don't understand metaphors unless they are hit over the head with them.'

'*Do you have an alibi?*' She successfully fought the urge for an exasperated smile.

I didn't fight my urge to do likewise. The Cheshire cat had nothing on me.

Ten minutes later and the superintendent was back and not looking any more happy. Behind her was Sergeant Coker, looking a little uncomfortable.

I smiled at Susan Dean and held my hands out. 'Does this mean I am free to go?'

'If you don't watch it, Delaney, I will have you charged with indecent exposure!'

'And in possession of a dangerous weapon?'

Amy made a noise through her nose as she stifled

a chuckle and the sergeant smiled a little as Susan Dean coloured again. She glared at her colleague.

'And you can shut it as well, sergeant. You want to be careful of the people you decide to play pool with.'

She strutted away again as the sergeant handed me my mobile phone, wallet and keys.

I opened the wallet and took out a ten-pound note. 'That's what I owe from the game last night.'

Sergeant Coker trousered the note and gave me a thoughtful look.

'Quite a coincidence that you turned up in my local last night about the time Bill Collier was being done over.'

'I don't shed any tears over Collier. Do you, George?'

The big man gave me a thoughtful look once more. 'The super has got her eye on you, Jack. You've put her nose well out of joint. I'd step careful if I were you.'

I grinned back at him. 'Sure, Michael Flatley learned all he knows from me.'

'Maybe, but Superintendent Dean will have you dancing to an altogether different tune if you give her a chance. Keep your balls out of her hand is my advice.'

Outside the air was brisk but the sky was still clear. Amy Leigh walked beside me as I looked at my phone. I had missed a few calls from Henry at the golf club and one from Kate.

'Why were you winding Superintendent Dean up, Jack? You could have just told her you were with her sergeant last night. Seems like you were rubbing her nose in it, in more ways than one.'

'It's pretty simple. I don't like the woman, Amy. She did nothing to help the old lady and told me to back off.'

'And?'

'And I don't do backing-off.'

Amy shook her head in a fair impersonation of Susan Dean. 'Do you work on your routine on a daily basis?'

My phone trilled. I looked at the incoming number and answered it. 'Jack Delaney. OK, Henry, give me a few and I'll be there.'

I closed the phone.

'Developments?' asked Amy.

'Someone broke into the golf club last night. Rifled through the secretary's office.'

'Anything stolen?'

'Not sure.'

'It's all go in Sheringham,' said Amy.

26

I drove my car over the level crossing and into the Sheringham Golf Club car park.

The trains hadn't started running yet. Apparently there was a Halloween-special train all this week and Siobhan had pestered me to take her on it. I had pretended that I had to be persuaded. Who doesn't like a steam train?

The flags on the greens had all been taken down. Even though it had stopped raining the ground had been so soaked that the course wasn't ready for use yet. The wind had changed direction, at least, and was blowing out to sea now, which meant it was warmer.

As I walked around the back of the clubhouse I could see that the workmen in the distance had already started constructing a new fence, some way in from the cliff edge. Solly Green, an elderly man who did odd jobs around the course and the town, was driving a small cart that was automatically picking up golf balls from the driving range that ran to the right of the building. I nodded at him as I walked by. He sketched a brief wave in response and went back to scooping up the practice balls.

Henry was in his office with his secretary, Jenny Hadley, an affable lady somewhere in her forties. She had a pleasantly rounded body, a short bobbed haircut and a twinkle in her eyes.

'I'll get you something hot, Jack,' she said, winking, and headed out.

The office had been turned over pretty thoroughly: pictures off the walls, drawers upended and their contents scattered, the desk overturned, cupboards forced open and the files piled on the floor. The trophy cabinet was open but all the trophies still seemed to be in there. It all looked pretty random.

'Those trophies worth anything?' I asked.

Henry nodded. 'A couple of them, yes. Old, heavy and silver. If you knew where to sell them you'd get a fair price for the scrap value alone.'

'Anything missing?'

'Hard to tell yet. We're just going through it.'

'How did they get in?'

'The door was forced.'

I looked across at the window. It had been untouched as far as I could tell. 'How did they get into the clubhouse?'

Henry nodded at me. 'Isn't that where you come in?'

'My job isn't all about asking the questions, Henry. But that sure as hell is a large part of it.'

'As you know, the members' entry keypad uses a numerical code. We change that code every so often, but at night it is switched off and the door is alarmed.'

'Who sets the alarm?'

'I do, or Jenny does. Or, if neither of us is here, the functions manager from the restaurant.'

The golf club had had a restaurant built as an extension to the clubhouse a few years back for events. It was also for hire, to generate revenue.

'Was there a function on last night?'

'No.'

'Who locked up?'

'Me. I had a lot to catch up with and spending all day yesterday with the council and the health-and-safety people and organising the fence and workers and new path, et cetera . . .' He sighed. 'Well, it's put me way behind schedule and this latest caper isn't helping any.'

'I can see that.'

Jenny came back in with the coffee and for the next hour I helped put the office back in order. Henry couldn't be sure if anything had been taken: the club secretary's office went back a hundred years or more and goodness only knew what had been put away in the back of the many cupboards. When we were finished it looked pretty much as it had always done, just a lot tidier.

Didn't make a lot of sense to me. If it was just more vandalism then why wasn't anything broken? The cabinet glass smashed, pictures slashed and so on? And if nothing had been taken then what was the motive? Unless the people who had done it were looking for something.

I guess the question was, had they found it?

*

Elaine James was sitting behind the small reception desk of the surgery in Weybourne where Kate was doing locum work.

She smiled as I walked in. It was a nice smile. She was in her late twenties, had a trim figure that didn't argue with her nurse's uniform, long curly red hair and green eyes that this morning seemed lively with mischief.

'Are you coming to my hens' night tonight, then, Jack?' she asked.

'I thought it was girls only.'

'I thought you could be the entertainment.'

'Oh yeah?'

'As far as I know the girls haven't booked a stripper, and I hear you do something along those lines.'

'I'm just a shy boy from County Cork.'

'That's not what Superintendent Susan Dean thinks.'

'Ah,' I said, catching on.

'Sheringham is a very small town. Word gets around, you know.'

'So it seems.'

'And what with Susan being divorced and single and all, it's a bit mean to try and tempt her. You're getting married next year yourself, after all.'

'I had my hands strategically placed and I was just following orders.'

'Would you jump off a cliff if she told you to?'

'If I was married to her I would probably have already done it.'

Elaine laughed. 'Kate is in her office, catching up with paperwork.'

'Cheers, Elaine.'

'And if you change your mind, we will be out and about in the usual pubs. You can surprise us if you like.'

'Not in this cold weather. I have a reputation to maintain, you know.'

I winked at her and headed through the narrow corridor towards Kate's office.

The baby was asleep in her cot. Kate was behind her desk. The snail was on the thorn and all was right with the world.

'Jack, we've got a problem,' she said.

Maybe I'd spoken too soon.

27

I sat down in the chair opposite Kate's desk. 'Shoot.'

'It's the house.'

'Go on.'

'Cousin Sam's putting it on the market. We're going to have to move out.'

'What's happened?'

'She's been offered a permanent position in the States. She's going to accept it. She wants to buy a property over there, which means she will have to sell her property here to finance it. Which therefore means we'll be out on the street. She's looking for a quick sale and the estate agents don't think she will have any problem with that.'

'It's a nice house.'

'It's a lovely house, Jack. Siobhan loves it. I love it, the baby feels settled there. I know you like it, too. It's a family home. Feels like *our* family home, Jack.'

She was calling me Jack a few times too often for my liking, and the baby 'feeling settled' seemed a stretch. I could see the way this was heading.

'Diane called me this morning, Kate.'

'Don't change the subject. This is important to me.'

'I'm not changing the subject. She reminded me that my sabbatical is going to finish soon after Christmas.'

'I know. That's what I'm saying.'

'Coming up here was only ever a temporary thing. We said we would see how it went.'

'You love it up here, you said so.'

'I do. It's lovely countryside, the air is breathable. Some of the natives are friendly.'

'It's perfect for Siobhan. After all she has been through. She needed to get away, you know that.'

I'll give that to Kate. She knew how to sucker punch. Helluva lot better than Bill Collier's work colleague, that was for sure.

'She's strong. You know that.'

'She's flowering up here. Made a lot of friends. She loves the school.'

Left, right. Snap to the chin. Relentless. She was like Rocky Marciano.

'We have time to talk about it. Nothing's decided, is it?'

'We don't have time. Sam has spoken to her lawyers, so the clock is ticking.'

'There are other houses. We can rent meanwhile.'

'I want that house, Jack. We all do.'

Rock. And a hard place.

28

'Go on, Nigel. Jäger bombs all round.'

The guy being shouted at while standing at the counter in the lounge bar of The Lobster was Nigel Holdsworth. Or the Reverend Nigel Holdsworth, to be precise. Except he wasn't looking very reverend-like at that moment. He was in his late thirties, a tall, fit-looking man with blond hair and an accent straight out of Hooray Henry's diction classes for people not capable of speaking quietly. The group of friends with him were cut from the same cloth. Corduroy in pink or red, mainly.

I was sitting at the corner of the bar, pretty much minding my own business and letting the noise of the party wash over me. I knew a few of the guys in the group to nod to them passing in the street, but that was about it.

It was a stag party. Kate was out with the hens. We had got a babysitter to mind the kids and I was having a quick pint before heading home to relieve her and cook a bit of dinner.

I raised the freshly poured pint of Guinness to my lips when the hooray reverend jostled my arm and caused some of it to spill on the counter. I looked across but he didn't say a word, simply handed some shot glasses over to a friend who had come to collect them. I took a deep breath and forced a mental smile and lifted my glass once more. Once more he jostled me. Once more he didn't say a thing.

'Excuse me, Reverend,' I said in as calm a voice as I could manage.

'Yes?'

He gave me a puzzled and somewhat disdainful look. Much like a senior prefect might have given to a lowly fag in the public school he had no doubt attended.

'I know you are a man of God. But if you fucking nudge me again I will make sure you meet him a lot sooner than you intended.'

'And who the bloody hell are you?' he asked, red-faced with indignation.

'I'm a man who is trying to have a quiet pint and not get jostled by an arsehole out of his dog collar.'

His pal, a large man of the same age with curly dark hair, stepped around the reverend and came up to me.

'Why don't you shut the fuck up, you Irish—' he said and pushed my shoulder with his arm. I am not sure what the noun would have been had he finished what he was saying, but I surmised it wouldn't be flattering. So I stood up and punched him. A straight snap to the bridge of his nose, not enough to break it, but enough to knock him down on his red-corduroyed arse.

The other members of the party made a move towards me but a familiar voice called out from the corner of the room.

'All right, lads. A bit of horseplay is all right on a stag night. But let's not let it get out of hand, eh? You're getting married, Len,' he said to the man I had punched who was standing up and looking far from happy. 'You don't want to be walking up the aisle with a couple of black eyes, do you?'

'You think I can't handle him?'

'I think that I am an officer of the law and I have just given you some good advice.'

Sergeant Coker walked up to them with his hands held wide in a placating gesture, but the expression on his face made his meaning clear enough. The groom was glaring at me, but the reverend took his hand and led him away.

'Come on, down these and let's get off to The Crown,' he said, polishing off his shot. 'There is a very unpleasant reek of the black Irish bog in this bar this evening.'

The unhappy bridegroom hesitated at the door and then pointed a finger at me.

'You'll keep,' he said and left with the rest of the party.

The sergeant joined me at the bar. 'You can't go around just punching people, Jack' he said.

'Sure, it was just a tap.'

'Get me a pint of Fosters and a pint of the black stuff for the fighting Irishman, please,' he said to the blonde-bobbed barmaid behind the counter.

'You going to behave yourself, Jack?' she said to me.

'I'll do my best, darling. But I'll just stick with this pint – I'm driving home in a wee while.'

She smiled and went off to the other bar where the Guinness and lager taps were.

The sergeant gave me a thoughtful look. 'You boxed a bit?'

I nodded. 'For the Met.'

'Like I say, you can't keep going around punching people, Jack. It's frowned upon in some quarters.'

'I noticed.'

'And he's a nasty piece of work, that Len Wright. I'd watch your back if I were you.'

'Isn't that what you're here for?'

'Next time I might not be.'

I nodded and sipped my beer. 'I'll try and be careful.'

Harry Coker laughed. 'I guess you can take care of yourself.'

'Sometimes.'

The sergeant pulled an A4 envelope out of his bag and laid it on the bar.

'What's this?'

'Something you didn't get from me.'

'And what is it that you haven't given me?'

'The autopsy report from Norwich on our John Doe.'

'Anything of interest?'

'Not sure. Still don't know how long he was in the ground. I figured you could run your eye over it. More your area.'

I nodded and pulled the envelope towards me. 'Cheers, Harry.'

'Figured you'd get hold of a copy through Kate sooner or later.'

I nodded again. It was exactly what I had planned on doing.

'So I also figured sooner would be better than later,' said the sergeant.

29

It was a cold night. Neither of them noticed. The blood in their veins was pumping with alcohol and excitement.

They were in a back alley which ran off a small passage that itself led from the high street past an amusement arcade and through to residential streets. It was relatively dark in the alley: the lights from the amusement arcade had been switched off, and the couple's warm breath in the cold air was barely visible.

The woman had been positioned against a stone wall. The man behind her lifted her dress. She had a warm coat on but no knickers – as she had been instructed.

The man behind her unzipped his fly, his excitement all too obvious to her. She giggled.

'Oh my,' she said. 'I hope you have a licence for that.'

The man slid his hand between her parted legs and whispered in her ear.

'Somebody seems to be ready for it,' he said.

'Are you going to fuck me or talk me to death?' she replied and then grunted as the man acted upon her question. 'Jesus!' she gasped when his stomach slammed against the top of her buttocks as he entered her.

'No blasphemy,' the man chuckled as the woman juddered against him, the heat from her bottom arousing him even more as he gripped her hips and pulled her towards him.

'This is the last time,' the woman gasped, breathing raggedly.

'We'll see about that,' he replied. Her long hair fell over her face as she leaned further over the wall and he slapped hard into her in a regular rhythm.

It didn't take him long and, spent, he sagged against her, both of them breathing deeply, gulping in deep draughts of the cold night air.

The man removed the L-plate sign that was pinned on the back of her coat and tossed it to the ground. 'I guess you won't be needing that now,' he said.

'Jesus!' gasped the woman again.

Neither of them noticed the man in the dark shadows further down the alley, who was watching them with eyes as cold as the night air.

30

William

The moon was in full sail in the clear night sky. A few clouds scudding across it, but certainly not enough to obscure the vision of the man who approached the wall of the grounds of All Saints Church in Beeston Regis.

It was a low wall, built many, many years ago. The man put a hand on top of its weathered stone and flint and clambered over it into the cemetery beyond.

He was carrying a torch in his pocket but in the bright moonlight he had no need of it. And he knew exactly where he wanted to go.

He moved quietly, stealthily. But in truth there was no need for him to do so. The nearby caravan was empty at this time of year, and the nearest houses were several hundred yards away back on the Beeston Bump. The church had no rectory and was unoccupied at night, and the people in the graveyard were unable to voice outrage at what the man had come to do.

He walked around the side of the church until he came to the grave that he was seeking. It was a decorative grave with a black granite headstone and stone borders. The top of the plot had been filled with white quartz.

The man read the engraving carved deep into the stone and he murmured, almost growled under his breath. Then he reached into the pockets of his thick warm overcoat for the other items that he had brought.

'One down,' he said, and smiled. His teeth, yellow in the moonlight, were as ragged as most of the headstones in the cemetery. There was a light in his eyes that came not just from the moon, a light as cold as that which fell from the dead rock in the sky above him and that illuminated his work.

31

The Reverend Nigel Holdsworth had what his mates at the golf club called a shit-eating grin spread broadly across his shiny face. He adjusted the zipper on his trousers once again, more from reflex than necessity, and buttoned up his overcoat – wool and cashmere mix and worth every penny of the hundreds of pounds it had cost him. He tightened his university scarf around his smooth-shaven and scented neck and walked back down the alley towards the lights. Maybe time for a few more in The Crown with the lads, before heading home for a glass of 18-year-old single malt and a very well earned night's sleep.

A figure stepped out from the shadows and Holdsworth blinked, surprised for a moment. But before he had a chance to voice that surprise a fist slammed into his stomach and the air exploded from him as he collapsed backwards in a gurgling heap. He tried to suck in air but found that he couldn't, the pain scaring him more than he had ever been scared in his life. His eyes watered and finally, thankfully, he was able to draw air into his tortured lungs. The tears springing from his eyes were as much from relief as from the agony in his stomach muscles. But he was to get a lot more scared – and soon.

The man leaned down and clapped a hand over his mouth. Then, holding him tight against a fence, he wound silver duct tape around Holdsworth's mouth. The priest's eyes flickered left and right. And then the man punched him on the side of his head and he fell to the ground like a sack of coal. The man lifted him over his shoulder as though he were more like a sack of feathers and headed back into the darkness of the alleyway towards his parked van, its back door open like a waiting mouth.

The priest opened his eyes slowly, closing them again as the pain in his head kicked in like a jolt of electricity.

He was bent over a church pew, he had seen that much. His mouth was taped tightly shut and he had to choke back the urge to vomit. His arms had been tied in front of him, and the cold draught told him that his trousers and underpants had been removed. God, no! He wanted to scream it out loud. He opened his eyes a crack – it was dark but the moon had sailed clear of the night clouds and shone pale through the coloured glass. He knew where he was. Tears pricked his eyes as a long thin blade was held against his neck.

The blade was removed and he hoped that his friend had forgiven him. It was only a shag, after all. Christ knew they had both shagged enough women. Had shared them. So she was getting married to him. It had just been a last farewell.

He felt large hands on his backside and tried to move his legs, but they had been tied too. He felt his buttocks being pulled apart. He looked up at the church's large crucifix, at the face of his saviour, cold now in the chill of night, and prayed to him as he had never prayed before. Not even forming words, just a desperate, agonised, silent pleading.

And then the man entered him and the Reverend Nigel Holdsworth let the tears stream down. From the pain, the searing brutal agony of it. And from the humiliation. An eye for an eye. A tooth for a tooth.

The man behind him grunted, slamming into him, pushing him hard against the pew, grunted as he himself had done some short while earlier as he had entered his best friend's wife-to-be.

One final grunt and the man pulled back. The priest's face purpled with pain, remorse and disgust.

He would never talk of it. That much was certain. The horror was over now and he would never speak of it to a living soul.

Except the horror wasn't over. It was just beginning.

32

Morning, and I was sitting at my desk, reading through the autopsy report.

Kate and I had gone through it the night before. She was handy that way – translating the scientific blah-blah-blah into comprehensible English. She made herself amenable in other ways, too. Of course, her enthusiasm the night before might have had something to do with her persuading me to stay in Norfolk and buy her cousin's house. Call me Mister Cynical. Either way, like the man who didn't care about the weatherman's forecast, you didn't hear me complaining.

Still, the report didn't add much to what we already knew. I flicked through the photos, looking at a close-up of the label that was in the man's suit. Sergeant Coker had told me that they had sent it off to be processed, to see if they could get the image any clearer, but it could take quite a while to get the info back.

I picked the photo up, slid it into a Manila envelope and put my coat on.

Ten minutes later Amy Leigh looked up in surprise as Laura Gomez showed me into her office.

'Jack, just the man I want to talk to.'

'Oh yes?'

'Helen Middleton informs me that your builder friend turned up to finish the job on her kitchen.'

'That's good.'

'Moreover, he says he doesn't need any further payment from her as you settled the bill.'

'In a manner of speaking.'

'Is this "manner of speaking" something I shouldn't know about again?'

'I think discretion is often the better part of valour, don't you?' I replied, fairly certain that she wouldn't wish to know that the costs were being offset by the sale of a Lexus car that was already probably somewhere in Europe.

'Least said, soonest mended,' she replied.

'Silence is golden,' chipped in Laura Gomez.

'As Thumper once famously remarked: if you can't say something nice, don't say nothin' at all,' I said, but not doing the full impersonation. A man has his dignity.

Amy Leigh held her hands up. 'OK, we've got the idea. Just so long as it doesn't come back and bite us.'

'I am pretty sure it won't,' I said.

'So what can we do for you, handsome?' said Laura, giving her eyebrows a touch of the gothic-vamp wiggle.

I pulled out the photo of the inside of the dead

man's jacket. 'I need this scanning into a computer and e-mailing PDQ.'

'What's a PDQ? I know what a PDF is,' asked Laura.

'He means pretty damn quickly!' said Amy.

Laura gave me an exaggerated salute and took the picture. 'Yes, sir! Mister Detective, sir! I is right on it.'

She left the room.

'So you haven't got a scanner in that high-tech office of yours, Jack?'

'I've got a printer but the scanner bit doesn't want to scan.'

'The room at the end here is available for rent. Just been speaking to Jane downstairs. Want to take it on?'

I considered it for a moment or two. A caravan in a farmyard, near the cliffs in the bleak midwinter. There was a view, certainly, and I wasn't just thinking of the stable girl. But then again an office in a warm brick-and-flint building, in the heart of town, with facilities on hand and a phone signal was pretty tempting.

'When can I move in?'

'Soon as you like.'

'I'll get my stuff.' Such as it was: files, a laptop, not much else. I figured I might leave the printer.

Amy looked at me, and there was amusement dancing in her eyes.

'Kate will be pleased,' she said.

'Oh?'

'Saw her last night at the hen do.'
'Did you now?'
'Oh, yes. We had a lovely chat.'
Women.

33

Sergeant Harry Coker was manning the reception desk of the police station. He was contemplating strolling over the road and getting a bacon sandwich.

He had missed breakfast that morning, and breakfast to Harry Coker was like the wind unto a mariner stuck in the doldrums. He found it hard to get going without it. He sighed as the door opened and a woman entered. A woman he recognised.

Emily Skipton. Spinster of some fifty-five years, general busybody and a continuing source of discomfort in the fundament of Harry Coker and others of the parish.

'Good morning, Miss Skipton,' he said.

'Is it?' she replied with a disdainful sniff and walked up to the counter, laying her neatly rolled brolly on the counter much as a judge might have laid down his gavel. If judges in this country still had gavels. Which they didn't.

'I certainly don't think it's going to rain.'

'I am not here to talk about the weather, young man.'

Harry Coker sighed inwardly once more. The

woman was not much more than a decade older than him but talked to him as if he was a truculent fourth-former or whatever they were called nowadays in the high schools.

'How may we be of assistance?'

'The Reverend Holdsworth is missing.'

'What do you mean, "missing"?'

'What do you think I mean?' she replied angrily. 'There is not much confusion about the word, is there? He is not at his church, nor at his house, and his bed has not been slept in. He is missing and I want to know what you are going to do about it.'

The sergeant bit back a remark that he was going to make about the reverend's sleeping arrangements being nothing to do with him. 'He was out with a group of friends at a stag party last night,' he said instead.

The woman's lips curled a little. She was the priest's cook and house manager at the rectory but, as in all other areas, she liked to think that her duties lay beyond those that were merely stated on her contract of employment.

'Do you mean to imply that the vicar, a man of God . . . that Reverend Holdsworth would have become embroiled in some kind of activity that . . . that . . .' The woman seemed unable even to contemplate the very thought of whatever it was that the sergeant might be implying.

The sergeant held his hands up in a soothing manner. 'Not at all, Miss Skipton. Just that the group of friends might have retired to one of their houses.

Maybe the groom's. Maybe they made a bit of a night of it and he crashed over.'

'Crashed over!'

'Stayed over.'

The sergeant had grown up in Sheringham. They had gone to different schools but he knew Nigel Holdsworth well. And he knew his friends. He might have a dog collar round his neck but Harry knew he was just following in the family tradition and was far from what you might call a saintly man. He wouldn't be at all surprised if they had all ended up in a night-club in Norwich, or hired escorts to visit a hotel and send Len Wright off to wedded bliss in fine carnal style.

He said none of this to Emily Skipton, however. When it came to her blessed Reverend Holdsworth she was the three wise monkeys all rolled into one.

'So what are you going to do about it?' she asked again, picking up her brolly.

The sergeant eyed the instrument suspiciously but somehow managed to summon up a reassuring smile that also indicated how seriously he was taking the matter. 'I shall make enquiries immediately, madam,' he said. 'Round up some troops if necessary. Rest assured that if the Reverend Holdsworth has come to any harm we will find him.'

'Young men do foolish things on stag nights, silly pranks. Maybe he is tied to a lamp-post somewhere.'

'He's not the groom.'

'What?'

'Well, it's the groom they usually tie to lamp-posts or suchlike.'

'When alcohol and young men get together, sergeant, there is always a danger of foolhardiness and I should expect you to realise that better than most.'

Emily Skipton turned and walked out, a galleon in full sail. The sergeant wondered whether she had been referring to him personally in her remark about alcohol and foolishness or had simply meant that he as a policeman had witnessed the behaviour concerned. He didn't consider it for longer than it took for the door to close, however. He had an appointment with a hot bacon roll or two that he didn't intend to miss. He waited for a minute or so then headed for the door himself.

The Reverend Holdsworth would turn up shortly, he had no doubt, with lipstick on his dog collar and a smile on his public-school-educated, smug and shiny face.

34

I was just loading the last of my office paraphernalia into the boot of my much maligned Saab when the sound of sirens approached once more.

Technically it was just one siren and one police car. The siren mercifully stopped as the car pulled alongside my own. Sergeant Harry Coker got out on the passenger side and a tall young uniform with ears like jug handles got out on the driver's side.

'Sorry about the twos, Jack,' said the sergeant. 'Young Gary here wanted to have a play with them.'

The young uniform, somewhere in his twenties, smiled. He had large teeth that, unlike the rest of him, weren't entirely uniform.

'Got to give the locals something to gossip about, haven't you?' he said.

'What can I help you with?'

'The super wants you cuffed and brought down to the nick,' said Harry Coker, shrugging apologetically.

'Again?'

'Seems that way.'

'Do you reckon she's got the hots for me?' I asked the constable who surprised me by blushing a little.

'I wouldn't know about that,' he said.

'I think Gary here has got the hots himself for the boss, Jack,' said Coker. 'Woman in power, wouldn't be the first time.'

'Rubbish!' said Gary, blushing even more and laughing far from convincingly.

'So what have I done now?' I asked. 'Speeding, parking on a kerb, walking up the street in the wrong direction?'

'Not exactly.'

'That guy Len Wright. I guess he's laid a complaint against me?' I asked. In truth I had been half-expecting it. I was surprised that he hadn't come after me with his fists later that night. He seemed the type.

'No, Jack. The Reverend Holdsworth has gone missing.'

'What's that got to do with me?'

'And so has Len Wright, the bridegroom.'

'And . . .?'

'And it has become known to Superintendent Susan Dean that you were involved in a fracas last night.'

'A fracas?'

'Her vocabulary. She also knows that Len Wright threatened to see you some other time and sort you out.'

'And so she assumes what?'

'She thinks they might have ended up meeting you again and found that they were boxing below their weight as it were.'

'I left you and went home, put the kids to bed and stayed up for a couple of hours reading before going to bed.'

'Kate with you?'

'Kate was with the hen party. The lucky lady who is getting to marry Len Wright works as a nurse at their practice.'

'I know. Poor cow. Anyway, the super wants you in, official statement and all that. I am sure that Holdsworth and Wright will turn up soon enough. They're probably down the clap clinic, getting a shot.'

I held up my hands. 'OK, I'll come quietly,' I said.

'Sod that for a game of coconuts,' said Sergeant Coker. 'Bring your car. I hear you're moving your office into town anyway.'

It seemed that only the big secrets stayed hidden around here.

35

I was heading up to the roundabout at the bottom of Holway Road, following the police car ahead, when my mobile phone trilled.

'Jack Delaney,' I said answering it and steering with one hand.

'You do know it's an offence to drive and speak on a mobile phone, Jack?'

'Is it going to be added to the charge sheet, then, sergeant?'

'Slight detour. Follow us down to the beach.'

'What's going on?'

'I guess we'll see.'

I followed the police car as it swung down Beeston Road, then Beach Road, which led down to the sea. We turned slowly onto the promenade and made our way at a very sedate pace. We parked up behind another couple of police cars and walked down to the beach. The tide was coming in as the sergeant led me up to the site where the dead man's body had been found.

'What we got?' Sergeant Coker asked a man in a hard hat, behind whom was some earth-moving equipment and some other men in hard hats and hi-vis vests. After the forensic team had finished, these guys had been called in to clear the fallen cliff from the beach.

'Hi, Harry. What we got is something we didn't expect.'

He gestured us all forward. 'See here?' he asked, pointing to the remains of some chalk blocks at the base of the cliff.

'Yeah – we got a cliff, and we got what's left of the stuff that fell down that you haven't cleared yet.'

I walked up to the jumble of chalk blocks and ran my hand along an edge.

'These have been tool-cut.'

'Who's your buddy?' the man asked Harry Coker.

'Jack Delaney, meet Simon Brown,' he replied.

I held my hand out and shook his.

'You have a sharp eye, my friend.'

Coker laughed. 'Don't you know who this is? This is DI Jack Delaney. Poster boy for the Metropolitan police and darling of the press. Nothing gets past him.'

'What's a hotshot like you doing in these parts, then?' asked Simon Brown.

'I'm on a gap year.'

'He's taking a sabbatical.'

'And you're helping out while you're up here?'

The sergeant grunted. 'Technically, I am supposed to be taking him in for questioning, so in that sense you could say he is helping us with our enquiries, yes.'

The guy handed me a torch. 'Get down and have

a squint through that gap,' he said, pointing to a space between a few of the blocks of chalk. I bent down and shone the torch as Harry Coker leaned down beside me.

'It's a cave,' Harry said.

'Certainly looks like it.'

'Your mystery man wasn't buried at the top of the cliff, he was buried under it. And then he was blocked in.'

'Yo, sergeant!' a voice called from along the beach near the promenade. 'You better get over here.'

Coker, myself and the young police constable walked back along the beach. The man hailing us was someone I recognised from The Lobster. A member of the lifeboat crew and a local electrician. His name was Ian Hart but everyone called him Spike, because of his spiky hair that hair-care products seemed unable to control. A tall man in his late forties with a broad Glaswegian accent.

'You'd better get here, Harry,' Spike called again.

The sergeant picked up on the urgency in the man's voice and we quickened our pace.

'He's at the slipway, bottom of Beach Road.'

'Who is?'

'Not sure.'

A few minutes later and our cars had headed back down the promenade towards Beach Road again.

A fishing boat was pulled up on the beach. The net beside it on the slipway was empty of fish but had something else in it.

A human body.

We walked over and looked down.

'We saw it on the water,' explained one of the fishermen. 'Thought it might be a seal or dolphin at first, then we realised.'

He opened up the net and the naked corpse flopped on its side. Male, in his thirties, with skin the colour of eight-week-old milk. The smell was not too fresh either.

It was the Reverend Nigel Holdsworth. Late, I guess, of this parish, as they say.

'You better get out of here, Jack,' said Harry Coker.

I nodded. 'I'll go up to the station and give them my statement.'

'Might want to call your wife on the way.'

'Super Susan's not going to hold me.'

'I wouldn't put it past her. But no. I meant we might need Kate down here.'

'I think this guy's beyond the benefit of medical attention, Frank.'

'Still, nice to get a jump. Cause of death. Norwich are going to be on this like white on rice.'

I nodded. 'I'll make a move.'

'Jack,' he said as I went over to my car which was parked now on Beach Road.

'Yes?' I looked back at him questioningly.

'You ain't brought a lot of luck to our town, have you?'

36

Kate and I were sitting in The Ship at Weybourne.

It was another decent bar, one that hadn't been totally made over into a pub-themed restaurant. They did food but had a separate restaurant for the gastropods – as I like to call them – and a proper bar separately. I was having a club sandwich. It was good. Kate was tucking into a BLT, and none too daintily. One of the things I liked about her was that she looked like a model, sounded like the well-educated doctor that she was, and ate like a hungry field worker. A woman of appetite. My kind of woman. My woman, in fact . . . and that put a smile on my miserable Irish face pretty much every waking day.

She put her sandwich down and took a sip of diet Coke. 'So they're not going to charge you?'

'No,' I said after swallowing the last mouthful of my sandwich. 'Although I get the impression that nothing would make Susan Dean happier. Short of a multiple orgasm and even then it's a toss-up.'

Kate frowned. 'I'm not sure I am happy with your choice of phrasing, Jack.'

'You're a doctor, Kate. You should know about these things.'

'I meant the fact that you choose to associate the woman with a sexually based comparison. To say such a thing indicates it is possible, and maybe probable, that you have had such images in your mind.'

'Then put such thoughts from your own mind, cherry pie. Jack Delaney is a one-woman man. He has seen the light, oh Lord. And the light is shining from your big brown eyes.'

'Did you just call me "cherry pie"?'

'I certainly did. My one and only cherry pie.'

'Well, that's OK, then.'

'She can't charge me with assault. Enough witnesses were there to prove that I was acting in self-defence.'

'And were you?'

'No. But that's not the point.'

'And now the Reverend Holdsworth is dead and the best man is still missing.'

'Yes.'

'That's why I called you.'

'Go on?'

'I need some advice.'

'Advice of what nature?'

'Supposing a girl was about to be married.'

'A girl like you?'

'Well, not like me, exactly. Let us say a more adventurous sort of girl.'

'Adventurous in an outgoing kind of way?'

'Maybe just in the going sense.'

'As in a goer?'

'You are more down with the vernacular of the street, darling. But yes. Promiscuous, shall we say, or sexually experimental.'

'This girl was going to be married soon?'

'Yes.'

'And she works with you?

'You are quite the detective.'

'I just follow the clues like a bloodhound. And when I have eliminated the impossible then what remains, however improbable, leads me to conclude that a nurse in your employ has been getting up to the naughties.'

'Naughties?'

'Indeed.'

'Anyway, she is not in my employ: she just works with me. But yes, she *has* been getting up to the naughties – as you so delicately put it.'

'In Ireland you learn to be careful with phrasing – as you put it – or you get hit on the arse with a wooden spoon.'

'I shall have to remember that.'

'So Elaine the hen has been wandering away from the cock, as it were?'

'I can see that they didn't use the spoon enough on you, Jack.'

'The Brothers had harsher techniques. Would "stag" be a better term?'

'It would.'

'And it has relevance, you think, to the death of Nigel Holdsworth?'

'Nigel Holdsworth was stabbed before he was put

into the sea. I was able to determine that much before the Norwich crew arrived to take charge.'

'As you said.'

'So I need some advice as to whether I should go to the police.'

'About what?'

'The hen. Elaine. Marrying Len Wright. Apparently she wasn't just seeing the vicar for spiritual advice.'

'He was diddling her?'

'Charmingly put.'

'They were having an affair?'

'Maybe your description is more accurate. I don't think it was a love affair as such.'

'So the Reverend Holdsworth has been stabbed and the groom-to-be of the fiancée whom he was diddling would seem to be a prime suspect.'

'That's your area of expertise, darling.'

'So what is the dilemma?'

'Maybe he didn't do it. Do we ruin her life by giving out information that may have no bearing, as you legal types say, on the case?'

'A man has been murdered.'

'And no doubt the police will be interviewing everyone who attended the stag night, much as they did you. They are bound to talk to Len Wright, too. Maybe we should wait?'

'They would speak to Len Wright, I am sure, but . . .'

'But?'

'They can't find him. It seems that the groom has gone missing, too.'

And then Kate's phone rang.

37

The Norfolk and Norwich Hospital is south of Norwich and about an hour's drive from Sheringham.

But it was the closest A & E to Sheringham and the ambulance would have taken more than an hour to get to us. In Kate's car, with me driving, we made it in about forty minutes.

Elaine James had been a pretty woman. She certainly wasn't that now. Someone had used her like Mike Tyson used to use a punchbag. She was sedated and sleeping at least, her fractured ribs bandaged up, a splint across her nose and her jaw wired. Her closed eyes were black and swollen. I had seen my fair share of violence to women in my job, but still felt sickened at the sight of her, and hearing the sound of her ragged, wet breathing.

I wasn't quite sure how she had managed to call Kate. She had her on speed dial, I guess. All Kate could hear when she answered the phone was the quiet, desperate whimpering of somebody in great pain. Thank God for caller ID.

Kate had tended to her injuries as best she could and I had carried Elaine as carefully as I could to

Kate's car. I had tried to ask her for details of who had done this to her – although, given the circumstances, I had a strong suspicion – but she was unable to speak and Kate had insisted that I should drive. She had bandaged Elaine's jaw but immediately on reaching the Norwich and Norfolk A & E. Elaine had been fast-tracked into theatre and her jaw was now wired. She wouldn't be speaking anytime soon.

We were slipping into our overcoats when two suited men approached us, holding out warrant cards as they did so.

'Detective Inspector Rob Walsh,' said the first man. About five foot eight, in his early fifties and with a lean, spare frame, thickish-looking black-rimmed glasses and a receding hairline.

'Sergeant Swift,' said his partner, whose name was probably the cause of some hilarity. He was taller than his boss, wider and about twelve stone heavier. He had a cheerful ruddy complexion, short-cropped blond hair and he reminded me a little of a younger Harry Coker. Who knew, maybe they were related. Either way, neither of them was smiling at me and neither one offered his hand.

'You'd be Jack Delaney,' said DI Walsh.

'I would that,' I replied.

'Doctor Walker, nice to meet you,' Walsh said to Kate and smiled extremely briefly.

'OK. What can I do for you?'

'I'd like to speak to you alone – if that is all right?'

'No, that is not all right. Although he is on sabbatical Jack is a serving member of the police force,' Kate said.

'He was questioned earlier regarding an assault on the boyfriend of this woman. The boyfriend is also missing.'

'Are you seriously suggesting that he stabbed a vicar, did God knows what else to Len Wright, and then beat Wright's girlfriend practically unconscious simply because some Guinness was spilled at a stag party?'

'He did punch Len Wright.'

'After provocation and in full view of plenty of corroborating witnesses. And no charges have been laid, have they?'

'Bit hard if the would-be complainant is missing.'

'Maybe he is missing because of what happened to his fiancée,' I offered.

'Meaning?'

'What do you think I mean? Look at the state of her! If he has done this, no wonder he is lying low.'

'And do you have any reason to believe he *has* done this?' Walsh asked pointedly.

Kate threw me a glance.

'Yes, I do.'

'And what would that be?'

'That would be that I am a detective inspector of the Metropolitan police force. The oldest and one of the finest police forces in the world and one I have been serving in for over twenty years. And when it comes to violence in the home, the first thing I look to is the partner because – as you know very well – that is the person who has committed the abuse in the large majority of cases.'

The DI swallowed and looked at Kate. 'Did she say anything to you?'

'No, inspector,' she replied. 'She wasn't capable of speech – she was barely capable of breathing.'

The inspector looked at me for a long moment and then finally held out his hand. 'Pleasure to meet you, Inspector Delaney.'

'Likewise.' I shook his hand, surprised at the seeming volte-face.

'Susan Dean can be a royal pain in the arse sometimes,' he said, clearing the matter up. 'But she's good police. All this is a little out of her comfort zone, shall we say.'

'Town mouse, country mouse syndrome.'

'Something like that. Either way we are on it now and I for one would be grateful for any assistance.'

'You got it.'

'I imagine it has been a bit of a change for you. From the the mayhem of London to the tranquil calm of the North Norfolk Coast.'

'A change for the better,' said Kate.

'And not so tranquil,' I added.

A vicious beating, an old murder, a recent murder and a missing suspect . . . North Norfolk was hardly my definition of tranquillity right now.

38

An hour or so later, after the inspector had recorded all the details we had given him, he had taken Kate and me to an entirely different part of the hospital.

A part where no healer can heal. A place where the human body has become evidence, a puzzle to be decoded. Injured flesh and bone a road map that led sometimes to the person who had committed the outrages and atrocities on their victims' corporeal forms.

I had never liked morgues.

The detective inspector had been talking to the forensic team who were working on the body of the late Reverend Nigel Holdsworth. I had stayed back by the door. I wasn't unused to such scenes, but after having seen what had been done to Elaine James I had no real desire to see a man opened up and eviscerated. Kate was an expert and it was Inspector Walsh's case so I was happy to take a back seat on this occasion.

Kate and the two Norfolk police came across to where I was standing. I had given up smoking but as we walked outside I had seldom felt so strong an urge to fire up a cigarette. I may not have witnessed with my eyes what the post-mortem surgical technicians had been doing but the odours had certainly reached me.

'Dead before he was put in the water,' said Inspector Walsh as we walked out of the morgue into the corridor and towards the exit door leading to the car park.

'Single stab wound to the chest. Pierced his heart.'

'We don't think he was in the water too long, either, so it looks likely he was held somewhere overnight.'

'Any idea of the weapon used?'

'Long, thin,' Kate said. 'And used with considerable strength – the blade exited the back of the rib cage, too.'

'He was run through,' added the inspector.

Kate looked at him thoughtfully as we walked along. I could see that something was on her mind but she wasn't ready to articulate it yet.

Twenty minutes later and we were coming off the ring road, heading down the Cromer road back towards Sheringham and Weybourne. I was driving but taking it at a more sedate pace. The sun was setting and the sky was blood red, streaked with clouds. Sunset by Hieronymus Bosch.

'My cousin Sam called me again earlier today, Jack. I was going to tell you at lunch.'

'Go on?'

'The estate agent has phoned her. He thinks he has someone very interested in the property. Might not even have to go to market.'

'I see.'

'Is that it?'

'Well. We would have to sell our own properties. That will take time. If Sam wants a quick sell there is not a lot we can do about it even if we did decide to stay.'

'I think we should. We can make a life for ourselves here, Jack. A good life for you and for me and for the children.'

'If we sell in London now we won't be able to go back, Kate. Property prices there are going up again. We'll be priced out of the market.'

'Is that your only concern?'

'It's one of them, yes, the main one.'

'Don't sell your property, then. Mine alone will raise more than enough to cover the cost of buying the house here. It's worth over three times the value. I am also not without other financial assets.'

'But you would have to sell it quick, you said.'

'Easily financed – my property in Hampstead will sell quickly and I can more than cover the costs of a bridging loan, even if we find that we'll need one.'

'You've thought this all through, haven't you?' I said, throwing a sideways glance at her. She smiled and nodded at me.

'I love you, Jack. I want this. More than anything.'

And there was the squeeze.

39

It was late afternoon. The sky black now, cloud-covered, and no moon.

I had moved my bits and pieces, such as they were, into the office that I had acquired next to Amy Leigh's. It was a nice enough room, at that: wooden floor with a rich rug, an old desk with a captain's chair behind it, a chair opposite for clients, a green wing-backed leather club chair in the corner for me to sit of a morning and read the *Financial Times* should I have the urge. I thought that would be unlikely. Old pictures on the wall of a nautical nature. An antique map of North Norfolk. All I needed, I thought, was one of those old globes that open up to reveal a drinks cabinet and I would be sorted.

I had locked up and was walking across to The Lobster when a drunken voice shouted out at me.

'Oi, Irishman!'

I turned round: Len Wright. Dressed as he had been for the stag night, unshaven, dishevelled and even more drunk than he had been then.

'Help you with something?'

'Yeah, you can help me. You can help me by fucking

back off to the stinking black bogs of Ireland where you crawled out from.'

He took a step closer to me, and put I put my keys in my pocket.

'I'm not a woman, Len. You come any closer to me and I am going to hurt you badly.'

'What do you mean?'

'Elaine James is what I mean. Made you feel more of a man beating her up, did it?'

He shifted his gaze sideways. 'I don't know what you're talking about.'

'Yeah, you do. Her and the Good Reverend. Your best mate. Didn't like the fact that he was shagging her, did you?'

He stumbled towards me and threw a roundhouse punch. I leaned back and caught his arm as it passed. I pulled him off balance towards me and smashed his head into a lamp-post. He grunted in pain and I pulled his head back and repeated the treatment.

'Delaney!'

I turned around and sighed inwardly.

'Let that man go!'

I did as Superintendent Dean asked. For some reason she didn't look to be in a good mood. Again. She had Sergeant Coker with her and a couple of uniformed officers. Len Wright slumped to the pavement, gurgling.

Seemed he had made a reappearance in town and had been getting rat-arsed in The Crown so someone had called the police.

*

A holding cell isn't a particularly interesting place in which to spend a long time and I was pretty much bored with the place after half an hour. The door opened, Kate was shown in and the door closed behind her.

'I've examined Len Wright. No lasting damage, but he's drunk, not fit for questioning. They're going to keep him in overnight.'

'Good.'

'And Superintendent Dean wants to do the same with you.'

'Not good.'

'Amy Leigh's speaking with her now. What the hell were you thinking of, Jack?'

'I was thinking he was swinging a punch at me and I didn't want to end up like his girlfriend.'

'You are more than capable of restraining him without smashing his head against a lamp-post, Jack, and you know it.'

'Seemed like a good idea at the time.'

'Why did you tell the superintendent about Elaine's affair with the vicar? I thought we agreed to wait.'

'Things have got a bit serious for that now, darling. And, besides, Len already knew.'

'How do you know?'

'I put it to him. I could see it in his eyes. He beat her up.'

'Hence the lamp-posting.'

'Hence indeed.'

'The White Knight syndrome.'

'A man should have a hobby.'

Kate sat beside me and ruffled my hair. 'What am I going to do with you?'

'Take me home and make love to me?'

'That door's locked, in case you hadn't realised it, Jack.'

I patted the bench we were sitting on. 'I know it's not the Ritz but it could make the time pass more pleasantly.'

Before Kate could reply the door opened once more and Amy Leigh came in. 'You got lucky, Jack. A couple of people saw the whole thing through The Lobster's window. They have made a statement to the effect that Len Wright attacked you again.'

'So I am free to go?'

'Not quite yet, Delaney,' said Susan Dean, who had appeared in the doorway. 'If you had information that Elaine James was having an affair with Nigel Holdsworth why did you withhold that information from my team and the team from Norwich?'

'I didn't have information. I had a hunch,' I said, looking her straight in the eye.

'Is that right?'

'Gut instincts. All good detectives have that. You know that, don't you, Susan?'

'What I know is that you are getting to be too much of a pain in the arse. I am still considering charging you with obstructing the course of justice. But I will be talking to your superiors and there will be a complaint made. I might not be able to charge you, Delaney. But I am going to make things very uncomfortable for you. You can count on that!' She walked away.

'Missing you already,' I called out.

'Jack!' Kate slapped my arm as we stood up.

'I reckon Len Wright is good for the assault on Elaine James,' said Amy Leigh. 'They'll question him officially in the morning, and Elaine will be able to confirm.'

I nodded. 'Good.'

'But he claimed he has been in Norwich with a woman since the night of the stag do. And the woman has confirmed it.'

'Who killed Nigel Holdsworth, then?' I asked.

It was a bloody good question.

Unfortunately, I didn't have any answers.

40

I was sitting behind my antique desk the next morning, pondering the matter, when Laura Gomez came into my office. Today she was wearing a black skirt, hooped tights in black and white, her trusty Doc Martens and a bright red woollen jumper. She looked like a liquorice allsort.

'All right, Bertie Basset,' I said. 'What have you got for me?'

She sat down in the green leather armchair and crossed her short but perfectly proportioned legs.

'I've come in to update you on the matter you asked me to look into, Gramps,' she said.

Gramps?

I let it slide. 'Get on with it, then.'

'Just had a call there's been some vandalism up at All Saints Church. Just up from the park, Beeston Regis. Want to take a squizz?'

'Sure,' I said, picking up my car keys from the empty desk and grabbing my overcoat.

It didn't take more than five minutes to get there.

It was a sunny morning. Crisp, clear air. The leaves were scudding gently in the light breeze as we got out of my car and walked round to the cemetery in front of the church.

Sergeant Harry Coker and his young sidekick were there ahead of us.

'Morning, Jack. They've released that scumbag out on bail, pending charges.'

'You couldn't hold him?'

'His alibi clears him for the murder of Nigel Holdsworth so even if he did know about the affair it wasn't him who killed the rev. But as soon as Elaine James is able to make a statement we'll bang him up soon enough.'

'Good.'

'Not so sure about that.'

'Why?'

'Plenty of people in this town have got no reason to like Len Wright. And there's plenty of people who like Elaine James. He'll be safer in custody, more's the pity.'

'So what's going on here?'

'A grave's been desecrated.'

It was an expensive-looking plot with a large marble headstone. The name and inscription had been crudely hacked away.

'Whose is it?'

'Don't know. Was hoping this man could tell us.'

He gestured at a tall, angular man who was striding purposefully towards us. He had longish silver hair and an overcoat. The dog collar gave me a clue about who he might be.

'Sorry, sergeant,' he said as he approached. 'Got stuck behind a beet tractor.'

'That's OK. You can see what's happened.'

'Terrible business. Disaffected youth, no doubt. But this is really reprehensible, desecrating someone's grave like this. It's barbaric.'

'Can you tell us who the plot is for, Reverend?'

'I'm sorry, I can't. I'm the vicar of the church in Upper Sheringham – I'm only covering for Reverend Harris. He's on extended leave.'

'Oh. So would anybody know?'

'I should think plenty of people do, but there is no need to put out an appeal. There will be a registry kept. I have the keys to the office.'

'I'll stay outside,' said Laura, producing a rolled-up cigarette. I followed the sergeant and the vicar into the church.

'This is Jack Delaney, a detective inspector from the Met. He's been looking into some cases of petty vandalism at the caravan park next door.'

'I would hardly call this petty vandalism.'

'No, no, quite.'

'Sometimes these things escalate,' I said.

A short while later and the silver-haired vicar had cross-referenced plot numbers with names and pointed to an entry in the book.

'Oh my word,' he said.

'What is it?' asked Harry Coker.

'It's that poor man's grandfather,' the vicar replied.

I looked over the thin man's shoulder at the entry in the book. Reverend Reginald Holdsworth.

Nigel's grandfather.

Outside, and the wind had dropped. It was warm, even. Warm enough to open my overcoat.

'Hey, Kemo Sabe!' Laura called over from a corner of the cemetery. 'We've got another one here.'

It wasn't as fine a grave as Reginald Holdsworth's had been. It was a plot set into the ground and it had a simple brass plaque. My eagle-eyed assistant had spotted that the name of the grave's occupant had also been gouged out. With angry strokes too, by the looks of it.

Back inside the church the locum vicar did his thing again with the record books and read out a name.

'William Wright,' he said.

'Billy Wright,' said the sergeant, clearly taken aback.

'You know him?' I asked.

'He was Len Wright's father. What the hell is going on here?'

It was another bloody good question.

41

I was back in my office, still pondering the matter and still not getting anywhere when Kate came in.

'What are you doing here?' I asked, surprised.

'Lovely to see you, too. Paperwork day,' she said, holding up a folder.

'OK.'

'And I've some to show you that you might be interested in.'

'Go on, then.'

She sat in the chair opposite my desk and pulled some photographic prints out of her folder. She put one in front of me.

'This is a close-up of the bone injury on our unknown man who was found in the cave under the collapsed cliff. The terminal injury, shall we say.'

I could see the hole that the weapon used had made in the dead man's ribs.

'Can you see the small triangular section of bone at the top of the entry point?'

'Yes.'

'That means that the weapon used had a groove in it. It wasn't completely flat like the blade of a knife or suchlike. And the groove had a purpose.'

'Which was?'

Kate smiled. 'Most people think it was grooved to let the blood flow more freely and allow the weapon to be pulled out quickly without getting stuck.'

'You're talking about a sword?'

'Go to the head of the class, Jack.'

'But the groove isn't there for that purpose I take it.'

'No. Just a bit of a myth – most experts agree now it was just to make the weapon lighter to use but still retain its strength.'

'So our unknown man was killed with a sword.'

'A small thin sword.'

'OK, so he was killed with a small thin sword. What does it tell us?'

'In itself, not a lot. But look at this.'

She handed over a second picture. 'The entry wound that killed Nigel Holdsworth, the fornicating vicar.'

'A similar nick. He was killed by a sword, too.'

'No, no, Jack,' Kate said and smiled briefly again as she put two even more enlarged pictures on the desk in front of me.

'It's just possible that he was killed by the same sword. You've either got a copycat killer or someone has waited thirty years or more to kill again.'

Superintendent Dean glared at me as Kate and I left the office that the Norwich CID team had taken over at the Sheringham police station.

She had heard of the developments and wasn't

happy that I was in the loop. Surprise, surprise. But there wasn't really a lot that she could do about it, especially as Detective Inspector Rob Walsh had let it be known that he had asked for my assistance.

'Where is he?' she asked as the reception doors opened and Sergeant Coker and a couple of uniforms came in.

'We can't find him,' he said.

'Well, bloody get back out there and look. Get more bodies if you need them.'

'Where from?'

'Give Yarmouth a shout. Use your initiative. He might not have killed Nigel Holdsworth but that bastard damn nearly killed his fiancée!'

'She's made a statement?' I asked.

'She responded to questions, though she's not able to speak properly yet. But yes, she has confirmed that it was Len Wright who attacked her. You should have hit his head harder against that lamp-post, Delaney. Might not have to be looking for him now if you had done!'

The superintendent stomped back into her office, closing the door.

I watched her go. I didn't care for her attitude but she had a damn fine derriere.

I probably wouldn't tell her, mind.

42

I was standing by the printer while Laura Gomez plugged in a memory stick and pushed some buttons.

'I should teach you how to do this yourself,' she said.

'All looks a bit high-tech to me.'

'What, they don't have computers and printers in that there London? Not even at the Metropolitan Police?' she said, pronouncing the last two words with a gushing awe that I found as convincing as a promise from a local politician.

'No, what we have are junior police officers and assistants who do it for me because I have got far more important things to do.'

The printer whirled into life and disgorged a piece of paper. Sally Cartwright had pulled a few strings for me and got the technology wizards at the Met to see what they could do with the image of the label on the inside jacket of the man in the cave.

They had done quite a bit. There was presumably the man's name – which was still illegible – but beneath some indistinct letters there were a few clear ones. Hxxtxn & MxxxS TxxxxRS

Laura looked over my shoulder at the printout. 'What you got there?'

'The label of the man in the cave's jacket. Just have to work out what it means.'

'Hoxton and Mears. Tailors. Norwich,' she said.

'How the hell do you know that?'

'Amy's uncle gets his suits made there. It's quite well known.'

'Do you mind if I borrow your assistant for a while, Amy?' I asked as she came out of her office.

'Not at all. I've got a meeting with a client for a couple of hours. We can discuss a fair splitting of her salary payment later. Pro-rata basis, I guess.'

'Hang on – I'm employing her now?'

'You've got to think of the future expansion. You have a young family to support now, Jack.'

'I'll want a rise,' said Laura Gomez.

Hoxton and Mears was a very old and long-established tailor's, or gentlemen's outfitter as they preferred to be called, on Timber Hill in the cathedral city of Norwich. Timber Hill itself was very old and long-established as well. It had a square-cobbled street and inset flagstones rather than raised pavements. I pulled up outside the shopfront and turned the engine off.

'You can't park here,' said Laura.

I put the *Police on business* sign behind the windscreen and opened the car door.

'And that's another thing,' she continued as she got out on the passenger side.

'What is?'

'This car has got to go.'

'Why?'

'It's all about appearances, Jack. It's very important in our game.'

'Is that a fact?' I said, locking the car.

'Darn tooting!' she agreed. 'You've got an office now, an executive assistant. That heap spoils the image that we present.'

'I wasn't aware I had hired a management consultant.'

'I am hired, then. That's good. Come on,' she said and held the shop door open for me. 'Let's crack this case.'

Edward Prout, the head tailor of Hoxton and Mears, was himself ancient and established, if not quite as much so as the premises or the street outside.

He was examining the blown-up photographs quite closely. 'Yes, this is definitely one of our labels,' he said. 'But I am afraid I am at quite as much of a loss as yourself about the name of the gentleman who commissioned this article.'

I pulled out another photograph, one showing the jacket after it had been removed from the dead man's body.

'Could you tell from this when the jacket was made?'

He looked again and shrugged. He was a little man with white hair and a natural tonsure. It made him look almost gnomelike.

'It is a simple country jacket. It's a classic design,

inspector – you could go back to the beginning of the last century and see it, and you could also buy one close enough to it from us today.'

'Pretty much as I figured.'

'Perhaps if you could get me the buttons. It might throw some light.'

I nodded. It had been a bit of a long shot, anyway.

Outside in the street I would have walked back to the car but Laura held my arm. 'Let's get a bite first.'

There were two pubs side by side just along from the outfitter. One was called The Murderers and the other was called The Gardener's Arms. I was going to open the door of the first one as we walked down the hill but Laura shook her head.

'I much prefer The Murderers,' she said and I wondered at her smile until I walked in the door. It was an old pub that had been built around 1530, was still family-owned and was full of different spaces – or nooks and crannies as they liked to call them. I could also see that this and The Gardener's Arms was in fact all one building, with two separate entrance doors and signs. Hence Laura's smile. Her little joke.

Sitting at the bar I sipped on a half-pint of the ale named after the pub, whilst Laura enjoyed a Bloody Mary with the somewhat vampiric delight I had predicted a few days before.

'So are we on the case, boss?' she asked.

'Will you stop calling me that!'

'Would you prefer "Gramps"?'

'No, I would not. Might I remind you that I am going back to the police force in a matter of months.'

'I very much doubt that.'

'Mystic Meg, are you?'

'Kate doesn't want to go back to London.'

'Yes, I do know that, thank you, Sherlock.'

'And there are three women in your house, Jack. You're outvoted.'

I was beginning to feel that there were more than three women in my prospective marriage, too.

'So back to the case,' Laura continued, as if the matter had been settled. 'You have a murder that took place a number of years ago. You don't know how long. Nigel Holdsworth was murdered sometime in the night or early morning after the stag party. The same murder weapon has possibly been used. Somebody has defaced the gravestone of Nigel Holdsworth's grandfather, and Len Wright, the original suspect in his murder because the reverend was diddling his fiancée, has an alibi as he was busy beating up said fiancée at the time and then spending the night with a whore in our fair cathedral city.'

'So far so good.'

'So far so bad, I would have said. However, someone, maybe the murderer, has been defacing gravestones, first of a relative of Nigel Holdsworth and now of a relative of his buddy Len Wright who has since disappeared.'

'True.'

'So are the names on the gravestones being defaced as a way of ticking off the victims? Like a trophy?'

'It's possible.'

'Well, one thing's for sure, at least.'

'What's that?'

'You're not a local. You can't go on the Shannock killer's list. As you don't have any relatives in the cemetery.'

'What the bloody hell is a Shannock?'

'Sheringham born and bred. Third generation, technically.'

'Anyway,' I said, finishing my drink and smiling patronisingly at her. 'Len Wright is on the run from the long arm of the law, not from any Shannock killer, as you call it. He'll turn up somewhere sooner or later.'

43

The following morning and another early one at that.

I was with Sergeant Harry Coker down on the beach again. Superintendent Dean was thankfully nowhere in sight and was giving me a bit of a wide berth, apparently. She had phoned my old boss Diane Campbell but had not got quite the response she had wanted, according to the scuttlebutt that Harry had cheerfully passed on.

The council people who had been clearing the site had made a small entrance into the cave. There were barricades all around it and safety notices. The architectural engineer had stated that there was a very low probability of further collapse. It had been a confluence of extreme conditions that had caused the initial slide. Lightning striking the chalk blocks that had sealed up the entrance and been weathered and covered over time. Again, they were unable as yet to tell us how long. The cave, apparently, had been tunnelled into the cliff hundreds of years ago. One of a few tunnels, possibly, that had been dug back in the days when smuggling was a common occurrence on this part of the coast. Holland and continental Europe were relatively close across the North Sea, hence the history of raiding and invasion and smuggling going back more than a thousand years.

The sergeant had a torch in his hand and was showing me around the interior of the cave. It ran about fifty yards before it hit a solid wall of more chalk.

'This has been artificially built, too,' he said, playing his torch beam over the surface of the wall.

I nodded. There were cracks and lines showing where the non-uniform blocks had been assembled.

'Was it built before or after the dead man was walled up in here, though?' I asked.

'No way of knowing until we can cut through this wall.'

'Is that going to happen?'

'Not anytime soon and not until after a lot of red tape has been peeled away, that's for sure.'

'Health and Safety?'

'The modern mantra.'

I looked up at the roof of the cave, wondering how many thousand tonnes of rock and assorted glacial-deposit matter lay above us, and thought that the health-and-safety brigade might have it right for once.

We walked back through the cave towards the entrance. I was kicking the loose rocks aside when something caught my eye.

'This site been fingertip searched?' I asked.

'Not yet. Our resources are a bit stretched at the minute, as you know, Jack. We have a recent murder and a missing man to deal with as well.'

'Do you want to bag that, then?' I said, pointing to a fragment of card that had come loose from the rock. There was water around it. Presumably the rest of it had been washed away now that the wall had been breached and the spring tides had come crashing up to the cliff face.

Sergeant Coker crouched down, removed a small ziplock plastic bag from his pocket and teased the fragment into it. It was beige, about two inches wide on the straight and downward angles. The inner edge where it had been torn was crooked. Part of a red circle with the letters IAL remaining in a faded red on top of a blob and part of a solid hemisphere of something or other in the same shade.

'What do you reckon it is?'

I looked at the piece of card in the see-through bag and shrugged. 'It might be a clue. Might just be a piece of litter washed in on the tide.'

'If it's a clue I am buggered if I know what it means.'

I nodded. But something familiar about it tugged at the back of my mind.

We walked back out through the wall of chalk blocks that the deceased man had been buried in and back onto the beach. The tide was far out now. And another spring tide wasn't due until the full moon so the cave and whatever else was in it should be safe from the waters of the North Sea at least until then.

As we walked back up towards the West Promenade my phone made contact with the Vodafone signal once more and beeped in my pocket. I took it out and found that I had missed a call. I vaguely recognised the number but couldn't place it. I pushed the green telephone signal and listened to the dial tone.

When the woman at the other end answered, she could barely speak through her tears.

'Inspector Delaney, I need to see you.'

She broke down in tears again and her words were unintelligible. 'It's OK, Helen,' I said. 'I'm coming straight there.' I clicked off the phone and looked at the sergeant, deliberating for a moment.

'Fancy a trip out to Salthouse?' I asked him finally.

44

Helen Middleton had recovered some of her compo-
sure by the time we arrived at her place.

She was in her newly finished kitchen and handed
us both a cup of tea and led us back into her living
room. I had introduced the sergeant and she was
pleased that I had brought him along.

We sat down in the chairs that she indicated. Then,
as she sat down herself and placed her teacup carefully on a coaster, her puppy jumped straight into
her lap.

It was a relief to see him. I had been worried about
the dog.

Bruno could obviously tell that his mistress was
upset and seemed anxious to offer what comfort he
could.

'What's happened, Helen?' I asked.

'Your friend came round to finish off my kitchen.'

'Yes.'

'Completing the woodwork on the windows,
glazing them and so on, whilst colleagues of his . . .
I believe the expression is *made good*?'

'It is.'

'And a very good job he made of it, too.'

'Yes.' I wasn't quite sure where she was heading with this but she seemed, as before, reluctant to broach whatever it was that was worrying her.

'Have Bill Collier or his workmates been back, Mrs Middleton?' asked Sergeant Coker. I had filled him in on some of the background. Not all of it, of course.

'No, he hasn't. Inspector Delaney assured me that he wouldn't be and he has been as good as his word. They haven't bothered me at all. Of course, I have been away for a while, staying at a friend's cottage, while the work here was completed.'

'That's good.'

'So what's happened?' I asked.

Helen's eyes welled with tears again and it took her a moment or so before she was able to speak.

'The man they found blocked up in the wall of the cave – I know who he is.'

The young girl sat huddled on the cold bench in the underground room that the men had come and built in their back garden. She hugged her rag doll Jemima to herself – its eyes were almost as big as her own.

The man sat next to her and patted her on her knee.

'It's going to be all right,' he said but she didn't reply. She was shutting out the sounds of the screaming noises that still haunted her. It was a warm afternoon but she was shivering. A small lamp threw out some amber light into the darkness.

'Would you like some toffee?' asked the man.

The young girl shook her head.

'You're a big girl now. You're seven, so you don't have to be afraid any more.'

But the roundness of the girl's eyes testified to the contrary.

'Can you keep a secret?'

The girl nodded.

'It will be our special secret. I am going to show you something but you are not to tell anyone else. Not mummy or daddy or anybody.'

The girl nodded again.

The man pulled back his wrist and showed her the watch strap he was wearing. It was a watch she had seen him wear before, but now in the centre of the strap there had been inset a shiny new plate. The girl looked at it but could not read what was written on there.

'What does it mean?'

'It's Latin. Amor Vincit Omnia. It means Love Conquers All.'

45

The night sky was coal black as I drew the heavy drape curtains over the bedroom windows.

They were old, period windows, as they were throughout the cottage: very nice to look at, pretty rubbish at keeping out draughts. After I had gone back to the police station and left Harry Coker to brief Superintendent Dean and the posse from Norwich, I had picked Siobhan up from school and cooked dinner. When Kate came back with baby Jade, she asked me about my day and I promised I'd fill her in when the kids were asleep.

I climbed into bed and took a sip of a brandy and soda I had prepared earlier. It was a small shot of brandy, a large shot of soda. As the curly-haired Jewish man once remarked, the times were getting different.

Kate came in, bereft of make-up, her own long curly hair tied back. She was wearing a warm-looking but far from sexy pair of pyjamas. She still looked heart-meltingly gorgeous.

'Get in here, sex kitten,' I said, pulling back the duvet on her side of the bed.

'Sure, and where else would I be going?' she replied, giving a laughable impersonation of the brogue that I sometimes adopted for dramatic effect.

'Nowhere, I hope.'

'Well, you can count on that,' she said as she slid under the duvet. Something in the way she said it implied she meant more than she was articulating and I had a damn good idea what she was referencing. But I let it slide for the moment and kissed her instead.

'That's for you,' I said.

'So now, tell me what she said.'

'It's 1941, and Helen Middleton is seven years old. The war is in full swing. England is getting hammered. This part of the country particularly so.'

'I know that. I grew up playing amongst the pillboxes along the clifftops here, remember.'

'So, young Helen is lying awake at night listening to the screaming bombs being dropped from thundering bombers. The explosions tearing up the towns and countryside. Being dragged out of bed down to the air-raid shelter in the garden. Her father is away, her mother is an emotionally closed woman. The only reassurance in her life comes from her older brother.'

'And he was fighting overseas?'

'No, he was a chronic asthmatic, excused service. Twenty-nine years old, so quite a bit older than her. She was unplanned. He was a music teacher and like a surrogate father-figure to her in those desperate times.'

'I'm not sure that I like where this is heading.'

I took a sip of my brandy and soda and shook my head. 'No, it's nothing like that.'

'Go on, then.'

'One day she was hiding out in the shelter and still hearing the screaming bombs, but they were only in her mind now, in her memory. Her brother came to fetch her out, but she was terrified, traumatised. So he told her a secret.'

'Which was?'

'That he had fallen in love. He had met a young woman and they had fallen in love with each other. She had given him her dead father's watch, not expensive but of great sentimental value to her. He showed her the inscription on the band that he had had engraved and fitted on a strap for the watch. "Amor Vincit Omnia."'

'Love Conquers All.'

'Exactly.'

'Our man in the cave.'

'It certainly looks like it.'

'So why was it a secret?'

'She doesn't know. She doesn't even know the name of the woman that her brother met.'

'What was his name?'

'David Webb. He taught music at the local school, like I said. But he was also a member of the Home Guard and a volunteer on the Sheringham lifeboat crew.'

'So what happened? He just vanished? Something to do with this woman? A jealous husband, a protective father?'

'Helen doesn't know. Nobody knows.'

'He just disappeared.'

'No, he didn't. He was called out one night a few days after he had spoken to his sister. A fishing vessel in trouble at sea. It was a huge storm and he got thrown overboard as they went out to the stricken craft. Is it possible that the body you examined was that much older than you originally thought?'

Kate nodded. 'There are cases where bodies much, much older than that have been preserved, almost mummified. It depends, like I said, on the soil and the nature of the materials where it was buried. Like peat bogs, for example. Again, a lot of salt.'

'David Webb's body was never recovered. It never washed up on shore.'

'Well, it wouldn't, would it, if it had been interred among blocks of chalk and buried in a covered-in cave instead.'

'Unless it was a different man wearing his watch.'

'Unless that, of course.'

46

It was late October and Ashleigh Ryan definitely should have been back at school.

But he wasn't. School was the last thing on his adolescent hormone-filled mind. He was walking along the beach at Sheringham, heading towards the Runtons with a girl from his school who was in the year below him. He was a tall gangly youth with dark hair and a goth style about him that made him think that he looked like a hero out of a *Twilight* film. It didn't. Emma Brundle beside him, had curly red hair and was wearing more make-up than was recommended in the guidelines from Brussels. She was wearing a shirt that was too small for her but she thought it would make her look like a member of her favourite girl band. It didn't. And the fact that she kept her coat open to show the effect was probably not the wisest thing to be doing, given the weather conditions. But Ashleigh Ryan certainly wasn't objecting. He was sixteen, she was fifteen – and young Ashleigh had decided he didn't want to wait any longer.

There were plenty of nooks and crannies on this

stretch of the coast and Ashleigh, with a gesture towards the romantic, had brought along a couple of bottles of strong cider, a pack of fags that he had nicked off his older brother, and a blanket in a basket that his mum used for storing logs in the lounge by their wood-burning stove. It was cold out after all, even in the nooks and crannies. If Ashleigh was to take her cherry, as Emma called it, then some comfort was going to be required. She had lost her virginity about a year ago and had been with several other boys since but she didn't feel that the tall youth beside her needed to be told about those facts however.

The sun was out and even though there was a nip in the air it was a fine late-autumn day. There was a hint of woodsmoke in the air. Somebody not waiting a week or so until November the Fifth before lighting their bonfire. Ashleigh and Emma had planned to go to the fireworks show and bonfire at Cookie's field on that night. But before then business had to be taken care of, and Ashleigh was in as good a mood as he ever had been in his young life.

Further up the beach he spotted a football that had been washed in by the tide.

'Here, fucking hold this,' said Ashleigh, handing the basket to his inamorata, forgetting in his excitement the romantic role he had elected to play. In truth, every other word he uttered was usually an expletive.

'He shoots! He scores!' he shouted as he ran up the beach. 'Get in! Back of the net!'

He launched a kick at the ball, seeing the action

in his adolescent mind's eye as a penalty that Van Persie might have taken at Old Trafford. Except that the ball didn't move and Ashleigh went flying over the top of it, holding his ankle and shrieking in pain.

His shrieks were nothing compared with the screams of Emma Brundle as she reached the spot and realised what young Ashleigh had failed to notice.

The object was not a football at all.

It was a head. A head presumably attached to a body that was buried beneath the sand.

47

'Len Wright?' DI Rob Walsh was asking Superintendent Susan Dean.

'As close as I can tell. Yes, looks like him,' she replied

'How long have we got before the tide comes back in again?' I asked.

'About four hours,' the expert among us, Sergeant Coker, answered. He was a volunteer on the Sheringham lifeboat, much like David Webb had been seventy-three years ago.

The Norwich DI signalled to a forensic crew who were standing by with trowels and shovels.

'OK, guys, let's get him out of the ground.' Flashes went off as the men and women in light blue protective suits swung into action again. Video footage was shot and the slow process of getting Len Wright out of the cold sand began.

'Was he alive when the tide came in, do you think?' I asked Kate.

'I hope not,' she replied. 'But we'll soon find out.'

I glanced down at the murdered man's head. His

mouth had been taped closed but his nostrils left clear.

I certainly hoped so, too.

Two hours later and we were sitting with the team that had assembled in a two-storey function annexe at The Lobster pub. The police station in the Tesco car park wasn't big enough to hold the amount of personnel that had been drafted in. Superintendent Dean was unhappy with my presence but I had officially been seconded to the Norwich team now, and was even being paid for it. She didn't like that much, either, but the wishes and desires of Susan Dean were as the idle winds that passed me by and troubled me not, as the Bard had once said – or something very similar.

Detective Inspector Walsh was leading the briefing, although there were more senior officers present. The media had gone into a feeding frenzy over the story and the small coastal town of Sheringham had been swamped with reporters. It was lucky, I guess, that it wasn't the height of the summer season. The beach had been closed and the town was practically under police law. To coin a phrase.

A noticeboard stretching across the room had been erected and various photographs, names, dates and timelines were displayed on it. There were probably about fifty people or so in the room.

'OK, here is what we know,' Walsh said. 'Last week a storm brought down part of a cliff, in the process exposing a blocked-up cave. A man had been buried in it and as far as we can determine at this stage that man's name is David Webb and he was murdered very late in 1941. The salt, soil and chalk conditions have preserved his body so that forensic analysis has been possible to determine the cause of death.

'Subsequent to an announcement of that discovery and an appeal for help in identifying the body a further murder has taken place.' He pointed to a photo. 'Reverend Nigel Holdsworth. Forensic examination shows that he too was killed with a small thin sword. Moreover, it is the same type of weapon that killed our man in the cave seventy-three years ago. Possibly even the same one. The main suspect in his murder, Len Wright, disappeared. He was the main suspect because he discovered that the not-so-Reverend Nigel Holdsworth had been having a sexual liaison with his fiancée. He beat his girlfriend brutally but had an alibi in the case of the second murder.' Walsh pointed to Nigel Holdsworth's photo again. 'Because he was holed up with a prostitute in Norwich at the time and the hotel staff back her alibi statement too.

'So far, so bloody strange,' he continued. 'Now Len Wright, cleared of the Reverend's murder, turns up. And forensic examination of his remains tells us a few things. He had recent contusions on his body. He had clearly put up a struggle. And from what local knowledge informs us Len Wright is known as a fighting man. So whoever took him was a very strong man. There is evidence of a single puncture wound. We are waiting for confirmation that it is the same weapon as was previously used and therefore whether the two or three murders are linked. Wright was buried up to his neck in the sand at night, with his mouth taped shut but his nostrils open so that he could breathe. Until the tide came in, that was.

'Moreover, someone scratched out the names of both these men's relatives from the gravestones at one of the local churches.

'This is clearly a dangerously deranged individual we are dealing with and to state the bleeding obvious we need to find him soon and shut him down.'

I tuned out as Walsh started listing areas of responsibility, who was doing what, who was coordinating the paperwork, et cetera. Something connected the three men, and that was the connection we needed to find. Maybe the stag night had something to do with it. Had something happened that we didn't know about? Something before Len Wright went on the rampage?

I had an idea of where to start looking.

48

Alice Featherton-Brightly was a leading light in the Sheringham Historical Society. She also worked in the local library, which was where I tracked her down the following morning. She was surprised to see me.

'Jack Delaney – what can I do for you?'

She was a mature lady with an accent of pure polished crystal, but she still managed to put a sexual connotation into the most seemingly innocent sentences.

'I need to track down the members of a lifeboat crew. During the war.'

'David Webb's crew I take it?'

'Yes.'

'You should be speaking to Helen Middleton.'

'I know that he was her brother, but she was seven years old at the time.'

'She's writing a book. On Sheringham in the war years. Not fiction.'

'Oh, I see.'

'She didn't tell you?'

'She mentioned that she was writing something.'

'She's borrowed the society's archives. If it was on a piece of paper she should be able to tell you.'

'Cheers, darlin',' I said.

'You can make it up to me another time,' Alice Featherton-Brightly replied, smiling and raising one perfectly formed eyebrow.

'Count on it.'

It was another fine late-autumn day and leaves were still clinging on some of the trees as I took the familiar coast road once again. So familiar that my car could almost have been put on auto-drive.

Helen Middleton was pleased to see me. She showed me through the lounge, into the now warm kitchen and down to the study area that she had made with the addition of a desk, a chair and a filing cabinet or two. Better equipped than mine.

'Please excuse the mess,' she said, pointing at the neatly stacked piles of paper on her large wooden desk.

'Not at all,' I replied. 'If you saw my office today you would be horrified.' Which wasn't entirely true: most of my pending paperwork of reports or quotations was still just that. Pending. Everything else had been put on the back burner.

'I am not sure if it's worse knowing that my brother was murdered. I always thought he died a hero's death.'

'Maybe he did.'

'But I am glad we have his body now, at least. We can lay him to rest with a proper ceremony.'

'We?' I asked.

'Oh, there's only me – my husband died some time

ago. He was older than me by several years when we got married. I suppose "we" is me and the puppy dog nowadays,' she said, pointing to her small dog who was curled up in a big padded pod and resting comfortably. Dreaming of rabbits and sticks and other pleasant things, no doubt, and who could blame him?

Helen pulled a faded newspaper clipping from an old folder.

'I've kept this all these years.'

She handed it to me and I took it gently, laying it down on the table. The gist of the article was that although David Webb had never got to don a uniform and fight for his country overseas, he had died a hero's death, as his sister had put it. Taken by the cruel sea as he came to the rescue of a stricken craft. There was no mention of whether the attempt had been successful.

'Did the lifeboat crew manage to rescue the crew of the other craft?'

Helen shook her head. 'No. At least, they lost track of it. According to reports, the storm battered the lifeboat back – they didn't even sight the other vessel.'

I was beginning to suspect that maybe there hadn't been another craft in the first place. Maybe the lifeboat had never been launched.

'Do you remember why that cave was blocked in?' I asked.

'The town council blocked a number of caves on the front at the time. People would shelter there if an air-raid warning sounded while they were on the beach, but they were considered unsafe. A bomb dropping could cause them to collapse.'

Which, I thought, was more or less what had happened. Although it had been a lightning bolt, apparently, and not a bomb delivered by the Luftwaffe.

The two other members of the lifeboat mentioned in the report were a police sergeant named Tony Carter and a local banker called Henry Wilson.

I held up my mobile. 'Do you mind if I make a call, Helen?'

'Of course not – would you like to use the landline?'

'That's OK – I've got a strong signal.' I pressed speed dial and waited for the call to be answered.

'What's up, boss?' Laura Gomez answered cheerily.

'I need you to track down some people.'

'Shoot.'

'Tony Carter who was a police sergeant hereabouts back in the 1940s and a banker called Henry Wilson, likewise.'

'Still alive?'

'I wouldn't think so. I need to know what happened to them.'

49

I had stayed with Helen Middleton for a further hour or so.

I didn't learn much more but I think she was grateful to have someone to talk to. Someone who was trying to find justice for her much-loved brother, a brother whom she had missed for seventy-three years.

I was heading east again, keeping my eye on the curving, twisting road. My phone trilled and I pushed the button on the hands-free set.

'Speak to me.'

'Well, chief, I have some information. Henry Wilson was killed in 1942 in an air raid, leaving no relations. Tony Carter lived till retirement age and fathered a son, who in turn fathered a son called Robert Carter who has a dental practice in Sheringham.'

So much for my theory about the other members of the crew going missing around the same time as David Webb.

'Give me the dentist's address.'

'Sir, yes sir!'

Laura did as she was told, finally. I wasn't quite

sure how she had got on my payroll, so to speak. Mind you, Amy Leigh had had pretty much the same experience. Collusion, to my mind. Amy, Kate, Laura, Siobhan – all colluding to keep us in Sheringham. Thank God for Superintendent Susan Dean, I thought. At least that was one woman who would be glad to see my sorry Irish arse kicked back down to London. She would also, no doubt, be glad to do the booting herself.

William

The man smiled as he looked at the headstone. He put out a strong finger and traced the words, running its tip into the grooves. It was a fine headstone in the graveyard of an old Catholic church in East Beckham, a small village just outside Sheringham.

There were floral decorations at the corners of the stone and a verse from the Bible, an inscription in a flowing italic hand beneath the name of the dear departed.

He smiled again as he read the inscription.

And, ye fathers, provoke not your children to wrath: but bring them up in the nurture and admonition of the Lord.

EPHESIANS 6:4

And then he smiled once more, picked up the old and rusted sixteen-pound sledgehammer that he had brought with him for the purpose, and smashed the headstone into small pieces.

'Rest in peace, Tony Carter,' he grunted under his breath. Then he shouldered the sledgehammer and walked away.

I turned along Addlestone Road, a tree-lined residential street.

Robert Carter's dental practice was at the far end on the right. A finely built Edwardian detached house that had been converted into the surgery. There were five partners in the practice as far as I could tell from the nameplates set into the brick wall by the reception door. Robert Carter's was at the top of the list but I could see that that was probably on the basis of alphabetical order.

There were two women sitting behind the long counter in the reception room as I entered. One of them was in her fifties and was tapping, in a businesslike manner, on a keyboard, scowling at the monitor and paying me no attention at all. The other, a younger, happier-looking woman in her thirties held a finger up to me as she finished her call.

'Can I help you?' she said after hanging up.

I showed her my warrant card. 'I'd like to speak to Robert Carter, please.'

'Oh my God. Is it to do with the murders?'

That got the elder woman's attention. Her fingers

ceased their tip-tapping and she turned round to look at me, suddenly full of curiosity.

'It's just a routine matter,' I replied. 'Is he available now or is he with a patient?'

'He's gone out,' replied the older woman.

I looked at my watch. 'When will he back?'

'He didn't say.' The younger woman answered for her. 'He took a call about half an hour ago and flew out in a bit of a rush. He said to rearrange his appointments for the day.'

'Where was he going?'

'Didn't say.'

'Who was the call from?'

'A priest. Can't remember his name.'

I wrote my name on a piece of paper, along with my mobile-phone number, and put it on the counter.

'Can you get him to call me when he comes back?'

I was opening the door when the younger woman called out. 'Father somebody he was.'

A Catholic priest called Father somebody. Fancy that! I smiled in thanks and went out the door.

52

I spent the rest of the afternoon taking care of a few outstanding issues.

I'd had a quick meeting with Brian Stenson, the owner of the caravan park. The petty vandalism seemed to have stopped, no incidents for well over a week. Maybe the fact that I, and now Laura Gomez, whom Stenson had met, had been looking into it had scared off whoever it was. Either way the owner seemed happy enough, and I was happy enough to sign off on it too. Then I went back to the office. Checked my mobile for messages, as I had gone out of signal range for a while. But there had been no calls. I called Robert Carter's surgery again but he hadn't returned from his trip out. I asked for his mobile number but it cut into his message service when I dialled it, so I did as requested at the tone and left a message, asking him to call me and giving my own mobile number. I tried to sort out some paperwork, but I was distracted so I soon gave up and headed to The Lobster. It was dark now and the wind was whipping off the North Sea hard enough for me to zip my jacket up to my neck.

The makeshift CID incident room in the double-storey function room of the pub was abuzz with activity as I entered. Lots of people talking on phones, lots of people typing on laptops. I had a word with a female police constable on DI Walsh's team but they were no further forward than they had been the last time I had checked in with them.

I tracked Harry Coker down having a bacon sandwich and a half of lager in the lounge bar. The landlord had closed that bar off to the general public and more particularly to the press who had descended on the town like a plague of biblical insects.

'Making any progress?' I asked as I slid onto the bar stool next to him.

'I am with this sandwich,' he said as he finished it with a large bite and chewed thoughtfully. 'But that's about all.'

I gestured to the barman and ordered the same for myself and another half for the sergeant.

'I tracked down the people manning the lifeboat the night David Webb was murdered – tracked 'em down on paper, obviously,' I told Coker.

'What were your thoughts?'

I shrugged. 'Loose threads. Pull at enough of them and sometimes the mystery unravels.'

'Is that what they teach you at Hendon?'

'It sure as shit wasn't needlework classes, Harry. I can tell you that.'

'So did you learn anything?'

'Well, either David Webb was lost at sea and the man in our cave was just wearing his watch. Or . . .'

'The men who said he was lost at sea were lying?'

'Exactly.'

'So what has that got to do with the murders here this week?'

'I don't know. But they happened after David Webb turned up after all these years very much not lost at sea. I went over to speak to the grandson of one of the men in the boat. The only surviving relative: Robert Carter. He's a dentist here.'

'Yeah, I know. He's on the lifeboat crew too.'

'He was out. I've left a message. Long shot, but I don't know. Maybe his grandfather told him something. Or his father.'

'What?'

'I have no idea. But that's what we do, isn't it? Ask questions because we don't know what the answers are. Get enough answers and sometimes things start to make a bit more sense.'

'So you're pretty sure that none of what has been going on here in our own century is coincidental.'

'No,' I said. 'I don't believe in coincidences like this. Somebody found out that David Webb was in fact murdered and not killed at sea when his body was uncovered. And is doing what, exactly . . .?'

The sergeant shrugged. 'Going after the people responsible? But they presumably died years ago.'

'That's why the gravestones are being vandalised. The sins of the fathers visited on the children. Is that the quote?'

'I don't know – the Bible's not my strong suit, Jack.'

I took a sip of my lager as Sergeant Coker's phone trilled. He answered it and grunted a few times. 'OK, boss,' he said finally. He closed the phone and looked at me thoughtfully.

'Your sandwich will have to wait a while.'

'What's up?'

'Catholic church in a little village just off the top road.'

'Yeah?'

'Another grave desecrated. The headstone smashed up.'

'We know whose?'

'Oh yeah – Tony Carter's. Your missing dentist's grandfather.'

53

You head south from the roundabout by the Sheringham steam railway and up the Holway road to get to what the locals call the Top Road or Cromer Road.

When we got to the T-junction there we turned left for Cromer, went a little way down the road and then turned right for the small village of East Beckham. It was farmland there mainly, with a few houses dotted around: no shops, no pubs, no restaurants but it still had a church. You couldn't throw a stone in this part of the world, after all, without hitting a church. Most of them dating back to the Normans when building them was a kind of hobby round here, I guess. Like stamp collecting.

The lights were on inside the ancient building of Saint Mark's, shining through the equally ancient stained-glass windows like an illuminated Christmas card. The Norwich police had got there a while before us and erected floodlights outside. The usual POLICE DO NOT CROSS tape had been put up at the entrance to the cemetery and a couple of uniformed officers were standing guard inside.

Sergeant Coker and myself ducked under the tape. DI Walsh was there with his sergeant and Superintendent Dean was looking, as usual, as if a wasp had stung her on her admittedly trim arse. We walked over to the smashed headstone and kept back as the crime-scene photographers did their thing.

'Looks as if you were right, Delaney,' said Rob Walsh – which didn't improve Susan Dean's mood any. 'If it is the same person and this is his calling card, then the modern murders are connected to the past and probably have nothing to do with the stag-night shenanigans.'

'Possibly,' said Susan Dean. 'And if it *is* the same person.'

'You got a lot of people going around smashing up headstones recently, Susan?'

'You know as well as I, Delaney, that there has been a spate of vandalism in the area lately.'

'In the caravan park. Some graffiti and minor damage. Hardly anything like this.'

'What's your gut feeling on this, then, superintendent?' asked DI Walsh diplomatically. 'I mean this is your territory, your patch, and I know we are sailing in uncharted waters here, if I may mix my metaphors. But what's your take on it?'

'Well, seeing as we are unable to contact Robert Carter, and nobody seems to have any idea where he is, then yes, we certainly have to consider the possibility that he has been taken by whoever was responsible for the deaths of Nigel Holdsworth and Len Wright.'

'The question is, what do we do about it?' I said.

The superintendent glanced at me, as though she didn't like my use of the word 'we', but I didn't much care. The time for petty local politics and power games was long gone. Had gone when David Webb turned up murdered after seventy-three years and buried in a cave, if you ask me.

'Something connects all these people,' added DI Walsh.

'Something that happened in 1941.'

He nodded, agreeing with me. 'We just need to find out what it is, before more names are chiselled out of headstones.'

I recognised a face over by the church entrance and left the official investigation forces to walk over and talk to him.

'How's it going, Solly?' I asked.

He grunted and muttered something in a thick Norfolk accent that I couldn't make out. He didn't seem too happy, was the gist of it. He was in his seventies, stooped but with a full head of long, still-dark hair that the wind was wrapping around his face. He used to be a fisherman so maybe the salt air had preserved the colour of his hair.

'You do the grounds here as well, then?'

'Yeah, voluntary.'

'Voluntary?'

'My church,' he grunted again.

'You see anything that happened?'

'No. And I just want to get home. Those people told me to wait.' He nodded dismissively at the police team.

'They take a statement?'

'No, just asked a couple of questions and told me to wait, like I got nothing better to do with my time.'

'Did you know the guy whose headstone was smashed up?'

'No, before my time. He was in the ground before I even came to Sheringham. I ain't a Shannock, you know.'

'Nor me,' I said.

He laughed at that, a short, bitter chuckle. 'No, I should say you aren't.'

'You see anybody looking around the graves?'

'Only her,' he nodded, scowling again at Superintendent Dean. 'Bloody bluebottle, telling me I got to wait.'

'Not tonight. I meant earlier.'

'Yeah, I know what you meant. She was here yesterday, having a look around.'

'You were doing the rounds yesterday?'

He grunted again. 'Evening Mass. We come out and she's there, peering at the graves.'

'She look at Tony Carter's grave?'

'Oh yeah. Bloody bluebottle.'

54

I was sitting behind my desk, waiting for Laura to bring me my morning cup of java and a croissant. Hell, if I was going to have staff on my payroll I might as well get some benefit from them. Maybe I should take a leaf out of Amy Leigh's book and get a glass panel in the door to my office and have DELANEY & ASSOCIATES etched onto it.

Outside the wind, as ever, was whistling, and the clouds were scudding in the sky like sailing ships. It was sunny, though. One of those rare breaks you get in England sometimes in October and early November, when it is bracingly cold but the light is bright – dazzlingly bright sometimes when the sun sits low in the sky. The sort of weather when wrapping a scarf round your neck, putting on gloves, duffel coat and hat and going for a long walk in the forests and kicking up leaves doesn't seem such a bad thing after all. Kate on one side, Siobhan on the other, the baby safely wrapped up warm in a buggy. Maybe a dog. A big mad enthusiastic Labrador to throw sticks for.

Damn, I thought, catching myself. I had better get back to London soon.

The door swung open, by virtue of a kick to its base from a small-sized Doc Martens boot and Laura Gomez entered, a large styrofoam cup of coffee in each hand and a paper bag clenched between her teeth.

She dropped the paper bag on my desk by opening her mouth, much as my imaginary Labrador friend might have returned that imaginary stick.

'None for Amy?'

'She's in court.'

'Oh yeah?'

'Some guy flashing his chipolata at a woman on the 9:45 Sheringham to Norwich.'

'Classy.'

Today Laura had dyed her hair purple, was wearing a leather jacket over a black Harley-Davidson motorbike T-shirt and a red skater-girl skirt over thick white tights.

'You got any electricity in your house, or do you just prefer dressing in the dark?' I asked her.

'What are you on about?'

'Just wondering why Amy never takes you to court with her.'

'Are you taking the piss?'

I took a sip of my coffee and shook my head solemnly. 'Not in my nature.'

'That's all right, then. So where are we on the case?' she asked, plonking herself into the chair opposite my desk and fishing out a croissant.

I filled her in on some of the latest developments. It actually helped to talk things through. Speaking aloud about something sometimes crystallises thoughts in your mind. They may have been floating around in your subconscious but sharing them with someone else can bring about a breakthrough.

It didn't in this case.

'So the dentist still hasn't shown up?'

'Not so far as I know.'

'So we can only conclude he has been taken by the killer.'

'That would seem to be logical.'

'So he is either dead, or is about to become so unless the police find him quick.'

'That would be a fair conclusion also,' I agreed.

'What's our next move then?'

'Our?'

'Well, Amy's not here. I thought we could go detecting and stuff.'

'What would you recommend?'

'I'd recommend we go back to All Saints Church in Beeston Regis, have a word with the verger and the groundsman and see if Princess Prissy has been poking her nose round there, too – and when.'

'Princess Prissy?'

'Susan Dean. The homecoming queen of the secret policeman's ball.'

'And what would that tell us?'

'That she knows more than she is letting on. That maybe she agreed with you all along. Or . . .' She shrugged.

'Or?'

'Something else.'

I had finished the croissant so I drained my coffee and stood up.

'Get your coat, then.'

'What coat?'

'Is that all you're wearing?'

'Yeah. It's not that cold. You is old is all, Stretch.'

She walked out the door and I followed, thinking it was about time I had a word with my personnel department.

55

The wind wasn't whistling any more – it was roaring now. Blasting in from the North Sea, stripping whatever leaves remained on the trees and scattering them through the air like large, autumnal confetti.

I had contemplated walking to the church but had taken the car instead and was pretty glad that I had.

I parked and turned the engine off. The vicar at Upper Sheringham had called the man responsible for doing the maintenance work and had arranged for him to meet us there.

It didn't take long for him to arrive. A tall, thin youth of about twenty-three came up and rapped on the window.

'All right, Laura?' he said.

'Eddie,' she replied, not too enthusiastically.

'You know him?' I asked her.

'Yeah, went out on a date with him once. It didn't work out.'

'Height issues?'

'Brain issues.'

I opened the car door and stepped out, almost

blown back a step by the wind. Open land ran from behind the church straight to the cliff's edge, and it didn't have to run far.

I held my hand out to the young guy and he shook it as though he didn't have much practice in such a ritual.

'Jack Delaney.'

'Eddie Peters.'

'So did the rev tell you why I wanted to speak to you?'

'Yeah, he said you wanted to talk about them two gravestones. Wright and Holdsworth, innit?'

'That's right. I wanted to know if you had noticed anything.'

'I noticed they were smashed up pretty good.'

'I meant before that.'

'Wasn't much to notice before then, was there?'

I was beginning to understand what Laura had meant.

'He means did you see anyone? You daft pillock,' she said, stepping in. 'Anybody suspicious, anybody looking around at the graves.'

'We get a lot of tourists here. They often come and look at the graves,' he replied. 'Me, I'd rather go down the arcade and play the slotties.'

'You had a lot of tourists recently?'

'Nah, it's well out of season, isn't it?'

'What about the superintendent, Susan Dean? You seen her up here, Eddie?' asked Laura.

'Only when she was here questioning us all. Bit like what you're doing, I guess. I reckon it's goths myself.'

I sighed.

'What?' Laura voiced her exasperation.

'Well, they're into all that, aren't they? Graveyards and cemeteries. Vampires . . . all that shit.'

'Well, you've been very helpful, Eddie,' I said, lying as I fished my car keys out of my pocket.

'Is that it, then?' he asked.

'Yeah, that's it.'

'What about the other one?'

'What other one?'

'The graveyard – another headstone's been chiselled out. I noticed it while I was waiting for you guys to get here.'

'Show me where it is, Eddie. Now!' I said, keeping a tight grip on my urge to plant a boot up his skinny arse.

He led us round the side of the church to another grave that had been dug near to the low stone wall.

It wasn't a well-tended grave, but again the marble was expensive and the masonry work was of a typically Victorian opulence and flourish. The name and inscription had all been hacked out of the marble by some crude tool. Most likely a chisel. Some of the gouges were deep so considerable force had been used to deface the stonework.

'Do you know whose stone this is, Eddie?'

The youth shrugged. 'No, I don't read them. Just push the mower round between them now and again. The vicar would know but he isn't here.'

'I know.'

'Is the church open?'

'It can be. I've got the keys.'

'Come on, then, you muppet!' said Laura, propelling him towards the church doors.

He finally managed to get the large oak doors open, I went through and up to the small office door but it too was locked. 'Have you got the key?' I asked and he shook his head.

'Don't worry, I brought my own.' I raised my boot and kicked the door hard, twice. At the second kick the lock splintered, the door swung open and I went over to the filing cabinet, pulling out the plot-number schematic and the log of names. It took me a moment or two to locate the name of the vandalised grave's occupant.

I felt the world tilt on its axis as I read what it was.

Jeremy Walker. Kate's grandfather.

Kate was at home with the baby that morning. Siobhan was at school. I pulled out my mobile phone and pushed the speed-dial button.

'Jack – how's it going, me big leprechaun?' she answered breezily.

'I haven't got time to explain now, but I want you to lock all the doors and don't open them for anybody. Even if you know who they are. Just stay there until I can get there.'

'What's up?'

'Just do it, Kate. I'll be home with you as quick as I can.'

Laura and I ran back to the car. I switched the engine on and sped down the hill, leaving a shower of gravel spraying back towards the very puzzled groundsman who was watching us go.

As I came back into Sheringham the traffic lights were just turning red. I leaned hard on my horn, overtook three cars who had pulled up at the lights and headed towards the traffic that was about to be oncoming. I got a few angry honks in reply but hardly heard them.

'Jesus Christ, Jack,' said Laura. 'Are you trying to get us killed?'

I ignored her and moments later I was pulling into Siobhan's junior school. I flashed my badge and was led to her classroom. Her teacher was a bit disgruntled by my sudden appearance but I didn't have enough time for niceties or explanations. Just said that it was an emergency and brought a far from unwilling Siobhan back to the car with me. Laura had climbed in the back to sit with her and I was back at our house minutes later.

Kate was waiting at the window. She went to open the door as Laura ushered Siobhan in.

'Jack,' Kate called to me as I walked back to the car.

'Go in and pack some clothes, Kate, for you and Siobhan – just for a few days for now. Laura will help you.'

She was about to say something but I held up my hand.

'Please, Kate. I'll be there in a minute.'

She must have heard something in my voice because she nodded and went back inside the house.

I opened the boot of my Saab and pulled back the spare-wheel covering. In the recess underneath was an oiled-leather package. I unwrapped it and took out a gun and a shoulder holster. I took off my coat and put the shoulder rig on, then donned my coat again and went in to explain to Kate.

56

Night-time in Sheringham.

It was bitterly cold. Yellow light pooling on the ground from sulphurous street lamps. Here and there kids and adults dressed in Halloween masks. Ghouls, monsters, witches, a woman in an Edvard Munch 'scream' mask.

The distant wails of police and ambulance sirens in cacophonous disharmony somewhere. Cars flashing past in both directions. I threw my cigarette out of the open car window a hundred yards shy of the petrol station. Moments later I pulled the car hard left and parked. Switching off the engine but keeping the radio on. Radio Norfolk was playing a sea shanty sung by a local group. 'Captain Stratton's Fancy.' *'Oh, some are fond of red wine, and some are fond of white, and some are all for dancing by the pale moonlight.'*

I stood for a while, breathing the cold, almost purifying air.

I holstered the petrol pump back in its cradle and turned round to see Superintendent Susan Dean standing there. She wore her trademark black wool suit. Her lipstick was the colour of fresh blood and her skin was the colour of the pale moonlight. Her eyes looked steadily at me, filled with contempt but also with purpose. A cold purpose. She held a shotgun in her hands and she raised it and pointed it at me. She was too far away for me to make a move towards her. I felt the beads of sweat trickle down from my forehead onto the bridge of my nose and into my eyes. I blinked to keep the moisture away.

I held a hand up in a calming gesture to stop her. But she shook her head, almost apologetically.

'Whatever it is, Susan, we can work it out.'

'It's "superintendent" to you – I've told you that. And it's too late for that, Delaney. Far too late.'

'It's never too late.'

'We're all born with a use-by date! You wouldn't be told. You wouldn't stop meddling.'

'I was just doing my job.'

'It wasn't your job. You wanted the truth so I guess you're going to find out.'

Before I could reply she had pulled the trigger. The noise was like a clap of thunder and I could feel the blood boiling in my ears now. The shotgun blast was like a burning iron fist in my gut. I cried out in pain and spun round and dropped to my knees. The shot had passed straight through me. Kate was standing there, holding her hands over her shattered stomach, with blood running through them like crimson rivulets. She had taken the full force of both barrels. She fell to her knees and smiled sadly at me.

Her eyes were peaceful and she seemed in no pain, but large tears welled after a second.

'It's all right, Jack,' she said. 'Take care of Siobhan and baby Jade for me.' And then her eyes closed.

I cried out and startled awake. My breath ragged. I was disorientated for a moment. I had no idea where I was.

'Was it the dream again, Jack?' Kate asked.

I took a sip from a glass of water that I had picked up from the bedside cabinet. 'Yes, and no. It was different.'

'In what way?'

I shook my head as if to clear the images that still lingered there. 'It doesn't matter. All that matters is that you're safe.'

After Kate had packed clothes for her and the children and supplies for the baby we had driven to the house of a friend of mine in Thornage, a small town just outside Holt. He was an ex-army man and ran a security firm based in Norwich. We had met over a contract we had worked on together.

I had explained everything to him and he had gladly taken us in, saying that Kate and the children were welcome to stay for as long as necessary. And, moreover, he would get enough personnel in to make sure that the house was guarded the whole time.

'Tell me about your grandfather, Kate,' I asked her.

'I never really met him much. My dad didn't get on with him. And when I went to live with my uncle in London he only visited a few times.'

'Did your uncle get on with him?'

Kate laughed harshly. 'Yeah – I think they were cut from the same cloth.'

'Would he know anything about what happened, do you think? Would his father have told him anything he knew about David Webb's murder and disappearance if he was involved?'

Kate looked across at me. 'From what I can gather he would have bragged about it to him.'

'He wouldn't have been alive himself when it happened.'

'No. But that wouldn't make a difference. My uncle used to let certain people know just what sort of a man he was and I bet his father was no different.'

'I'm going to see him.'

'When?'

I looked across at the clock. It was four o'clock.

'No time like the present. It's a long drive – the sooner I get there the sooner I can be back.'

'I'll come with you.'

'No, you won't. You'll stay here with the girls and keep safe.'

'He won't tell you anything, Jack. You know that. Even if he does know something.'

'It's worth a try. I'm not seeing you hurt, Kate. I can promise you that.'

57

Some hours later, and the dawn had finally broken.

I had taken Kate's car, partly because it had a full tank of petrol and partly because I didn't want my old Saab breaking down on me. Much as I hated to admit it, maybe Kate had a point about the car.

At that time of the morning I was able to make good progress: no idiots in 4x4s, no tractors or beet lorries. The A11 was mostly clear, as was the motorway when I hit it. Getting near the end of the M11, London was looming in the distance, the big urban sprawl of it lighting up the dark morning sky. The size and the spread of it as I hit the M25, which was busy with traffic by now, made me feel almost claustrophobic. Crossing the M25 and heading into the heart of the Smoke felt a bit like crossing the Bosphorus between Europe and Asia. It didn't feel like coming home, that was the strange thing. 'Never get out of the boat,' as Martin Sheen once said. 'Once you get out of the boat you ain't never coming back.' Or something like that.

A weak sun had risen in a milky sky by the time I left the Governor's office and was escorted by a couple of uniformed guards to the interview room where Kate's uncle would be chained and waiting for me. Diane Campbell hadn't been best pleased when I had called her shortly after four o'clock this morning but when I'd explained the urgency of the situation she had got straight on the case and made the necessary call.

Walker had changed a lot since I had last seen him. At the time of his arrest he had been a tall, upright man, exuding arrogance and authority.

As the door of his cell opened he looked at me with a sneering expression on his face. He wasn't arrogant any more – his flesh just couldn't suppress his thoughts. For years he had lived behind a mask, and now that the mask had been stripped away his features were mobile with his emotions. Hate, mainly, as he looked at me.

'Detective Inspector Jack Delaney, what an unexpected honour.'

He had been a fit man but he had gone to fat. His eyelids hooded his mobile eyes and he still bore the scar on his face from where Kate had slashed him with a knife. He had been abusing her and God knew how many other children over the years until I put an end to it. Given my way I would have put an end to him, full stop.

I sat in the chair opposite him. He had one arm manacled and chained to the wall. This wasn't at my request. I would have liked nothing better than for him to make a jump at me. But I hadn't come for the petty satisfaction of breaking bones in his puffy, sallow face. I had come for information.

'I know what you want, Delaney. Even though they refused to tell me anything.'

'Is that a fact?'

The manacled man smiled smugly, which given his situation was a neat trick to pull off. But he didn't pull it off with me. 'See, that was always your problem, inspector. Facts. As if truth was something immutable. Fixed. Right and wrong. Black and white. Well, in the real world there are no such things.'

'I didn't come here to discuss pseudo-philosophy with you, Walker.'

'No, you came here to talk about Kate and what is going on in the sleepy little seaside town of Sheringham. A town that has been rather woken up of late.'

I kept my face impassive. 'Go on.'

'But I've got nothing to say to you, Delaney. She's your damaged goods now. Nothing to do with me.'

I was tempted to get up, walk around the table and hurt him badly. But I could see that the thought amused him so I controlled the impulse.

'Oh, we get the television here, you know. I like to keep up with the news,' Walker continued. 'See what is going on in the world. The only pleasure I have left now that you have taken away my freedom.'

'I would have taken away more than your freedom, Walker. I'd have cut your balls off and fed them to you.'

'We're not so different, you and me. We both think the universe should bend to our rules.'

'That's where you are wrong. I am not at the centre of my universe. Kate is – and our children.'

He smiled again: a mockery of a smile, anyway. 'It's always a shame to see the centre of one's universe taken away.'

'Your father was involved with something that happened seventy-three years ago, Walker. What was it?'

'I have no idea what you are talking about.'

'You said I had come to talk about Kate with you, in connection with the murders. Now the only way you would know there might be a connection would be if you knew what that connection was.'

'I am guessing that Daddy's grave has been desecrated.'

'That hasn't been on the news.'

'Call it an educated guess.'

'Based on what?'

'Based on the fact that you have come scurrying down from your North Norfolk idyll to talk to me.'

'You will tell me what you know.'

'No, I won't. And you have no bargaining power. You have done all that is in your power to harm me already, Jack. You have no joker to play.'

'I haven't got a lot to lose, Walker. I could walk around this table and beat it out of you. The guards outside wouldn't do a thing.'

'They very well might and then you'd have everything to lose, Jacky boy. What about Kate? Poor little Kate would be left alone on the storm-battered cliffs. All alone with your young daughter and the wee bairn – doesn't bear thinking about, does it?' he said.

'You like your conditions here, do you, Walker?' I responded. 'Kept away from the general population.

Sharing your happy memories with the other kiddy fiddlers and nonces. How would you like to be moved away from them?'

'Not within your powers to make that happen, dear boy. I was a high-ranking police officer and, as you say, charged with crimes of a sexual nature against children. It would never happen.'

'Oh, I am not talking about moving you into the main wings, Alexander, dear boy,' I said, mimicking his pseudo-aristocratic accent.

'What, then?'

'I was thinking Berkshire.'

'Berkshire?'

'Yes. I don't think you belong in prison at all just now. You need help, Walker. That much is clear. The things you have been telling me now. Revenge-enactment fantasies. Surrogate, obviously. But the things you fantasise about doing to some of the other people here. Things with spoons and hard objects. I think you need a hospital until you are ready to be allowed to, shall we say, mingle.'

The smile had fallen from his face. He knew exactly what I was talking about. Broadmoor, the hospital for the criminally insane based in Berkshire.

'Six years or so under close supervision. Solitary confinement. Very limited access to television – your sole remaining pleasure, you said.'

'You can't make that happen, Delaney.'

'You said yourself that you were a high-ranking police officer. A major embarrassment to the Metropolitan Police. Much better for you to be declared criminally insane and tucked away in a padded room. It won't take much organising.'

Walker looked at me for a moment or two. I could see the fear in his eyes.

'I'm not telling you a thing, Delaney. I have no idea who is committing these murders. But if you want to know what's going on, why don't you speak to the police up there? They know more than you do. That's for sure.'

'What are you saying?'

He smiled again, the hate smouldering in his eyes. 'I've said all I'm going to say. Someone in that force certainly knows more than you. I guess you are going to have to find out!'

I kept on at him for a while longer but he wasn't going to tell me a thing. He was right: I didn't have any cards to play.

I'd been lucky on my run down to London. Not so lucky on my way back. The M25 was snarled up, almost in gridlock.

It took me over two hours just to get across it and up to Brent Cross and head north. The worst of it was, I knew no more now than I had before I made the journey. Walker was a nut that wasn't going to crack. He had something over me and he was going to milk that for all it was worth. I had to let it go for simple reasons, though. I didn't have time to lose, and I could tell he had made his decision. But I could tell something else. He hadn't been lying when he'd said he didn't know who the murderer was. He knew something about the death of David Webb seventy-three years ago and he knew that his father had been involved. But he had absolutely no idea who was committing the murders now: I could see that in his eyes and reading people was what I did best. Which meant that any background information he had on the wartime crime wouldn't tell me who today's murderer was. That was what I needed to know. And so I had left.

I picked up the phone and called Kate.

'Hi, Jack.'

'Everything OK?'

'Everything is the same as it was an hour ago when you called for the second time.'

'I need to know you are OK.'

'We're safe here, Jack.'

'Just stay there. I'm a couple of hours away.'

'We'll be fine. You just take care of yourself and drive carefully. The last thing that would help is you getting involved in an accident.'

'That's not going to happen. Give the girls a kiss for me and tell them I'll be back soon.'

I clicked off and pushed another speed-dial number.

'Harry,' I said as the phone was answered. 'It's Delaney. What have you got for me?'

'Nothing. Our dentist is still missing and the team from Norwich are buzzing around like a bunch of blue-arsed flies. But they have got nothing to go on. If it is connected to the stag party then maybe they'll have something to work on, but if there is no connection there . . . then they are back to square one. Meanwhile, who knows who the nutter is or what the hell he's up to!'

'He's not up to any good, sergeant. I know that much.'

'And Walker had nothing to give?'

'You heard?'

'I spoke to the superintendent. She was quite pleased to hear you were on a pointless mission. Glad to have you out of her hair for a while.'

I had briefed DI Rob Walsh as soon as I had left the prison. He seemed a bit put out that I hadn't told him earlier, felt that he should been there for the interview. But I wasn't going to worry about stepping on people's toes. I didn't have time. He accepted it, but I could tell he was far from happy. Antagonising the local police seemed to have become something of a hobby for me. But then again, as the fellow said, a man should have one.

'Where's Kate?' asked the sergeant.

'She's safe.'

'Where, Jack? We should be keeping an eye on her.'

'The fewer people know, the better, Harry. I'll check in when I get back to town.'

'Fair play.'

I hung up and slammed my foot on the accelerator just as a large crack sounded overhead and the skies opened.

It took me another two hours, as I had predicted, to get back to Thornage. I checked in with Kate every half-hour. Quarter of an hour out from the village I tried again but the signal was down.

I drove my car into the long gravel drive, ran up to the door and leaned hard on the bell.

The security guard opened the door. As soon as I saw the look on his face I felt the world slide away beneath my feet.

59

Siobhan came running up to me and hugged me round my legs as I came through the door.

'How long are we going to stay here, Daddy?' she asked.

I shook the rain from my hair and pointed at the window in the door. It was awash with streaming rain, and a thunder crack sounded in the air again as I did so, almost on cue.

'Do you really want to go out in this?'

She shook her head. 'Kate did, though. She said she wouldn't be long. She took the man's car.'

'OK, honey, you go and see that the baby is all right and I'll have a quick word with the man here and see you in a bit.'

'Sure,' she said and ran off into the lounge where I could see the baby asleep in her cot. I closed the door and turned back to the security guard who was looking at me, a little shamefaced, in the hallway. He was big, about six foot four and broad-shouldered, somewhere in his late twenties. I felt like breaking his nose with the butt of the pistol that was once again holstered under my jacket.

'Well?' I said instead.

'She got a call.'

'Who from?'

'I don't know. It was a woman. A patient. She said she had to go and see her.'

'And you just gave her your keys and let her go?'

'No, of course not.'

'So what happened?'

'I said I was under strict instructions not to let anyone out, including her.'

'And she went anyway?'

'She told me a patient's life was in danger. That she was seriously ill. I told her to call an ambulance but insisted that she had to remain in the house.'

I could imagine what Kate would have thought of that, but I had told her the same thing. I tried her phone again: no answer. I clicked off angrily.

'So how did she get out?'

'She called an ambulance. They said it was going to take a while. She seemed to accept it.'

I could tell that he was holding back on something. 'And . . .?'

His face flushed. 'I needed to go for a piss. My car keys were on the kitchen counter.'

'Jesus!' I said, my hands involuntarily balling into fists. 'And you can't remember the name of the patient?'

He brightened a little as he thought back. 'It was Ruth somebody. I remember her saying, "Calm down, Ruth. Try and breathe." After she answered the call.'

I pulled out my phone again. Maybe I should have

called the police but I didn't. I didn't like what Walker had been hinting at back in the prison interview room. I called Amy instead and told her to put Laura in a car to come and stay with the girls for a while.

'Have you got a shotgun?' I asked the security guard.

'The boss has a gun cabinet in the house. I know where the keys are.'

'A young woman about so high,' I said, gesturing, 'with purple or black or some kind of long punky hair will be here soon in a taxi. I want you to get a shotgun and stay by that front door. If anybody other than that girl, Kate, myself or your boss attempts to come through it I want you to shoot them. Do you understand.'

'Yes.' He nodded.

'Man, woman, police, I don't care. You pull the fucking trigger and keep pulling it.'

I went into the lounge to tell Siobhan that Laura was going to be here soon, and that I'd bring Kate back as soon as I could. She could pick up from my body language that something was wrong but she didn't know what. I did what I could to reassure her but I don't think she was convinced.

She knew fear when she saw it.

60

I ran through the pouring rain and jumped into Kate's car, pushing speed dial on my phone as I started the car's engine, slammed it into gear and tore out into the country lane that was running with water now. The car fishtailed and I righted it one-handedly as I gripped my mobile, waiting for the call to be answered.

God help any 4x4-driving muppet who got in my way.

The receptionist at Kate's surgery answered and I asked her for the addresses of any of Kate's patients whose first name was Ruth. She said she wasn't allowed to give out such information and I told her to put Ruth's colleague on. She would have fobbed me off at that but I explained in colourful Irish vernacular what I would do to her if she didn't get him on the phone.

'What's going on, Jack?' said Doctor Hugh Anderson, the senior partner at the practice. 'Lillian seemed very upset at the way you spoke to her.'

'Fuck Lillian,' I said. 'Kate's in danger, very serious danger. She has had a call-out to see a patient. I don't know if it is genuine or not.'

I could hear the phone muffling as he cradled it to his stomach and spoke with the distraught Lillian.

'It didn't come through here, Jack,' he said when came back on line. 'Maybe the patient called direct, which we discourage for obvious reasons.'

'It was a woman called Ruth – she was having breathing difficulties, as I understand it.'

'That's most likely Ruth Bryson. She only has a nephew who is elderly himself to look after her. Kate checks up on her once a week or so.'

'Where does she live, Hugh?'

'Weybourne. She has a caravan in a field on the right-hand side of the road by the entry to the beach.'

'I know it.'

'What's going on, Jack?'

But I clicked the phone off and punched Kate's number again. The message came back saying her phone was disconnected.

I switched mine off again, put my headlights on, peered as best I could through the windscreen wipers that were going at full tilt and floored the accelerator again.

I prayed that there was a God and that he was looking over us as I hammered through Holt, round the roundabout and then went as fast as I dared on the Cromer road. There weren't many cars out and it was easy enough to overtake any that got in my way. I went past the turning to the hospital, ignoring the thirty mph speed limit as I came to High Kelling, and then turned left. Downhill along a more narrow country road, flashing past Holt rugby club, through the woods and dropping down towards the coast. I came out eventually by the Weybourne church, another All Saints, fishtailed round another corner or two and headed for the beach.

My mind was racing. I was thinking about a man who had been stabbed and then thrown into the sea like slops from a bucket, about another man who had been buried up to his neck in sand, his mouth taped shut and exposed to an incoming unstoppable tide. And I thought of Kate in the hands of the madman who was seeking revenge on progeny of the perpetrators of a seventy-three-year-old murder.

I saw the field ahead. There was a large gate set into the wire fence surrounding it, but mercifully it was open. I could see Ruth Bryson's caravan. There was a light on inside. There was also a new-looking Volvo estate, the car that the security guard had described to me, parked outside. I took these as good signs as I screeched to a stop, jumped out of the car and rushed to the caravan's door.

61

I didn't bother knocking, just wrenched at the handle.

The door had been locked shut. I banged on it and there was no response. I popped the boot of Kate's car and got out the tyre jack. It was slippery in my hands but I managed to pry it between the door and the metal. It was an old caravan and it didn't take me long to force the door open, ruining the lock. A little job for a maintenance man but I was far from worrying about that. I climbed into the caravan.

A very elderly woman was lying on the floor but Kate wasn't with her. I threw open the door that led to a small bedroom and she wasn't there either.

The woman was breathing heavily and trying to say something.

'What is it, Ruth?'

But she couldn't manage to articulate what it was that she wanted to say. She lifted an arthritic hand and pointed a gnarled finger, its joints painfully prominent, and pointed towards the back window. Then her arm dropped and her eyes closed as if she was exhausted by the effort. She probably was.

I could hear an ambulance siren approaching, very

near now. I would have lifted the old woman onto the couch at the end of the caravan but I knew that could be the wrong thing to do.

'The ambulance is here now, Ruth. They'll take care of you.'

She sighed a wet sigh, small bubbles forming at the corners of her mouth. But there was a word in that sigh that I could just about hear. 'Kate,' she whispered.

I drew back the curtains and looked towards where she was pointing. There was a small cabin or large shed directly behind the caravan.

I went back out into the rain as an ambulance drove into the field. I picked up the tyre lever – slick with mud and rain now – from the ground where I had dropped it and walked around the caravan and up to the cabin.

It was a sturdily built wooden structure, locked and harder to get into than the old caravan had been. But finally I managed to wedge the tyre lever in and, using all my weight, finally got the door open.

I stepped inside, glad at least to be out of the driving rain. There was a light switch just inside the door and I flicked it on. No one was inside the cabin. Somebody had been, or was, living there, though. There was a single bed against one wall and a sink in the corner. Obviously the cabin was connected to the mains water. There was a neat table, with some paperwork on it and an old tin box. I looked at the photographs that it contained, old ones. If I'd had to guess I would have said they were from the early 1940s, before

David Webb had been killed. I knew that because he was in one of the photographs, and I knew *that* because his name was written beneath his picture, as were the names of other people in the shot. Names that I recognised.

They were standing on what was now the third tee at Sheringham golf course. Behind them was a large tract of open land. Nowadays there was a big block of apartments there that had coastal views. The fact that the men in the picture were all smiling at the camera and were not in any way dressed for golf made me think that the photo had some significance.

There were a couple more photos of David Webb, one of him with his arm around a much younger woman.

There was a letter in the box as well. I took it out and started to read it.

A minute later I put down the letter and was startled out of my thoughts.

'Excuse me.'

I spun round. There was a paramedic standing in the doorway.

'Are you related to the lady?'

'No,' I said, putting the letter and photographs back into the box.

'I need to take some details from you, sir.'

'Sorry, I haven't got time.'

I pushed past him and hurried back to the car, carrying the box with me.

'Sir!'

But I ignored him.

I knew most of it now. Knew what connected all the killings.

But I still didn't know where Kate was.

I drove out of the field, racing to get away from the paramedic who by now was banging on the car window. I headed back up the beach road and round the corner before parking at The Ship public house. I pulled out my phone and tapped in a number.

'Helen Middleton speaking.'

'Helen, it's Jack Delaney,' I said, trying to keep my voice level even though my heart was pounding in my chest.

'Nice to hear from you, inspector. Is there anything wrong?'

Everything was wrong. 'No, I'm just following up on some things that have come to light.'

'To do with David's murder?'

'Yes.'

'Well, of course – if there's anything I can tell you . . .'

'When I was at the cemetery the other day I noticed there were fresh flowers by his memorial plaque. Did you place them there?'

'No, it wasn't me, inspector. I've not been feeling at my best. I haven't been out of the house since my return. I have arranged for a proper burial, though, of course.'

'Of course.'

'Is there anything else I can help you with?'

I looked at the photograph of the men on the golf

course. There was one name I didn't recognise. 'I have an old photograph here taken on Sheringham golf course in 1938. There are four men in the picture. Your brother David Webb, Jeremy Walker, Reverend Holdsworth and a fourth man called Patrick Preston.'

'Yes.'

'I haven't come across the name Preston, but every other one I have.'

'Oh, the Prestons were a very influential family around here. Patrick Preston had a building development company with Martin Wright and Jeremy Walker. Poppyland Developments. I don't think the company exists any more but they certainly did a lot of building round here back then.'

'And was your brother involved?'

'He was for a time, but he sold his shares back to the company – not long before he died, apparently.'

'And did he make a lot of money on the sale?'

'Goodness me, no. There was a war on you know. And, to be honest, we were losing it at that time. I think that all he got back was his modest investment.'

'And what happened to the Prestons?'

'Oh, some of them are still around. In fact, you know one of them quite well, inspector.'

62

Kate Walker wriggled and squirmed.

Her hands were tied behind her back and her legs were bound at the ankles. She'd had a rag tied cruelly between her teeth and knotted tightly at the back of her neck, forcing her lips apart. Giving her a macabre rictus grin.

But her wriggling was in vain. There was no way she was going to get loose. Her eyes hadn't been covered, at least, but that was not much use to her. She was in some kind of hut and there was no light. She had tried shouting for help but the gag had made it impossible for her to make any noise above a low whimper. The wind was howling outside now.

Kate couldn't believe who had taken her and she couldn't believe what was happening, although it all too clearly was. The irony was not lost on her. She had been attacked in London before. Because of Jack's job. She had survived through her own actions but now she was powerless. She had persuaded Jack to move up to Norfolk so that they could all be safe. And now here she was, waiting to be murdered like the others before her. And she had no idea why.

She tried kicking out with her legs again but it was no use. She lay still for a while, her breathing coming in ragged gasps.

She didn't want to die like this.

And then she remembered what had happened to Len Wright and she had to fight to control her bladder. There was a creak as the door opened.

63

I had the phone on hands-free now and was driving back to Sheringham.

The rain had stopped. Blown over by the wind as suddenly as it had come. But that wind was getting stronger – I could feel it buffeting Kate's car as I headed down the twisting coast road. It was blowing straight off the North Sea again, its fury unabated as it headed southwards from Siberia.

'Amy, it's Jack.'

'For God's sake, Jack. Is everything all right? I've been trying to call you and your phone has been engaged or out of signal.'

'You know everybody in town, Amy, don't you?'

'Hardly. I know a few.'

'Do you know Ruth Bryson?'

'Not really. But I know her nephew.'

'Who is?'

'Solly Green.'

'Solly Green the odd-jobs man?'

'Yeah. You must have seen him – he does work up at the golf club.'

'Does she have any other relatives?'

'None that I know of.'

'What about Solly? Does he have any sons or grandsons?'

'Nope.'

'How do you know him, then?' I had to shout at the hands-free set because the wind was howling so loudly.

'Professional capacity, Jack. I've had to represent him a number of times.'

'On what charges?'

'Assault, affray, actual bodily harm.'

'He's an old man, Amy.'

'Don't let that put you off. He's as strong as an ox, Jack. Ask any of the police: it takes six of them to get him out of a pub when he starts scrapping – which he does often enough, even now. William Solomon Green is not a man you want to get on the wrong side of.'

'Where does he live?'

'With his aunt. Up in Weybourne in a field off Beach Road.'

I nodded.

'Where's Kate?'

'I don't know.'

I could see the golf club a few hundred yards ahead of me. 'I'm going to the golf club, Amy. I'll get back to you.'

I should have noticed the headlights in my rear-view mirror, but I didn't.

I clicked the phone off and when the entrance appeared I swung hard left into it, over the railway crossing, into the car park and over it onto the practice range. My car wheels spun in the soft mud as I gouged my way across the turf to the maintenance hut.

I jumped out of the car and ran to the hut. It was locked but I had chucked the tyre lever on the passenger seat of the car when I'd left Ruth's field and it didn't take me long to get it open. A locksmith was certainly going to have some work to do in the area. I flicked on the light and walked in. The place was piled with maintenance equipment: tools, paint, hedge-trimming shears. Old furniture. There was also a mattress in the corner and a bin full of empty vodka bottles and beer cans. There was nobody in the hut, though. I was about to leave when something under a stack of folding chairs caught my eye. I bent down to have a look and saw that it was the heel of a shoe. I pulled the shoe out and looked at it.

It was one of Kate's.

I slammed my hand against the frame of the door and looked out into the night. I was too late.

I stepped out of the hut, the wind rocking me. I looked up at the cliffs where it had all started seventy-three years ago. I pretty much knew it all now. Fat lot of good it did me.

My eyes blinked against the wind. I thought I had seen a dark malformed shape up on the hill, but when I blinked again there was nothing there. I started to walk towards it anyway. I couldn't afford to be wrong.

I had run a few steps into the wind when a familiar figure stepped out from the side of the clubhouse and blocked my way.

Bill Collier.

'I've been waiting for you, Delaney.'

'I haven't got time for this, Collier. Just step the fuck out of my way and you won't get hurt.'

He slid the baseball bat that he was holding down into one hand. 'I'm not the one who's going to get hurt, you Irish fucker!' he said. 'And I am going to do more than just hurt you.'

I sighed, pulled my pistol from its shoulder holster and levelled it at him.

'Like I say, I haven't got time for you, Collier. Back off now or I will drop you.'

'I wouldn't do that if I were you, Jack,' said a voice behind me.

I turned halfway round, still keeping Bill Collier covered with the pistol.

My mind raced back to what Kate's uncle had said earlier in the day. About the police knowing more than they were letting on. Remembering him saying it with a smile. Knowing something that I didn't. I had thought later that he'd been talking about Susan Dean. The fact that she was the granddaughter of Patrick Preston.

Right now, though, it was another police officer that I had to worry about. Standing there behind me was Sergeant Harry Coker, holding a shotgun in the business position.

64

I looked back at Harry Coker.

Calculating whether I had time to swing and fire my handgun before he had time to pull the shotgun's trigger. Not liking the odds but not liking the alternative, either.

'Do you know where Kate is?' he asked, puzzling me.

'No.'

'I saw some movement up on the hills. Get going.'

I didn't move for a moment.

'Amy told me you were here, Jack. For God's sake get going before it is too late! I'll take care of this bag of shite.'

I nodded and took off at a run.

I could hear Bill Collier's taunting laughter behind me as the sergeant approached him. I glanced back in time to see the laughing stop abruptly as Harry Coker smashed the stock of the shot gun straight into Collier's forehead. He dropped like a stone.

I carried on running. Thanking God for my new morning running routine and breathing evenly as I worked my way to the edge of the golf course and up onto the slope that climbed to the clifftop. I saw a brief flash of light ahead against the dark outline of the coastguard hut that sat on top of the hill. I pumped my legs, feeling the heat in my thighs, burning and tightening as my lungs fought to force enough oxygen into my bloodstream.

As I neared the top I could see Solly Green was waiting for me outside the hut, holding Kate with one large hand. He was standing upright now and for the first time I realised just how big he was. The moon sailed clear of the clouds as they scudded east and I could see that he had a feral smile on his face and a challenging look in his eyes.

'It's all over now, Solly. Let her go.'

'Not over yet, policeman. Not hardly.'

'I read the letter.'

'Then you know why it's not over.'

'Why didn't she take the letter to the authorities like David Webb asked her to?'

'Because she didn't know.'

'Didn't know what?'

'Didn't know what was in the letter. Because she couldn't read it. She weren't even sixteen yet. He didn't know the first thing about her. All he knew was to shag her and get her pregnant.'

'She was pregnant?'

'Yeah. He didn't know that, either. Turns out I'm a Shannock after all,' he said bitterly

'You're Ruth's son?'

'Yeah, and seventy-two years later she tells me it.'

'Let Kate go, Solly. This has nothing to do with her.'

'She's a Walker. She'll have to do.'
I pulled out the gun again.
'Let her go, Solly.'
'No.'
So I shot him.

65

He threw Kate to one side and charged at me.

I had shot him in the side and low. Mistake.

Should have shot to kill him. He was on me before I had time to fire again. He had an animal strength, I could tell that now. The strength of a madman. He wrapped his arms around me and slammed me to the ground. The gun fell out of my hand. I could see Kate's desperate eyes watching as we struggled.

His weight was crushing me and he raised his forearm to ram it across my throat.

I pushed up against him, trying to dislodge him. It was useless. I might as well have been trying to move a Mercedes truck. I couldn't breathe. I felt the pressure building in my head. Images flashing into it. My wife being killed at the petrol station. Flashes of shotgun fire in the sulphurous night. My daughter Siobhan sitting up in bed wide-eyed as I told her another stupid fairy tale I had half made up. Jade, our baby, a thing of wonder that Kate and I had made together. Pink, innocent, in so much need of love and protection. I thought of Kate. Beautiful Kate, with her laughing eyes and her long curly hair. And I pushed again.

Nothing.

The blood was pounding in my ears now, louder than the wind that howled and cried and wrapped itself around me like a shroud of pure energy. Then, suddenly, the blackness seemed to lift and a light bloomed in my head and I felt as though I was floating.

And then, with a rush, sweet oxygen came back into my lungs and I realised that the weight had been lifted from me. I stumbled to my knees and gasped ragged breaths deep into my lungs. I looked across. Harry Coker was standing face to face with Solly, exchanging blows. His shotgun was on the ground. I half crawled, half stumbled over to it and picked it up as Solly smashed a fist into the side of Sergeant Coker's head and knocked him down.

I stood up and levelled the shotgun at Solly as he stood at the cliff's edge. His hair fanning wild around his cragged face, his massive frame blocking my view of the sea behind him, the moon illuminating him like a biblical prophet in the throes of divine revelation.

'It's over, Solly,' I said, gasping the words, each utterance a painful rasp in my near-fractured throat. He shook his head and pointed at me.

'No, it is not over. For just as the Lord is slow to anger and abounding in steadfast love, forgiving iniquity and transgression, he will by no means clear the guilty. Visiting the iniquity of the fathers on the children, to the third and the fourth generation!'

'Yeah, I went to Sunday school too, you mad fucker,' I shouted back at him. 'But this is a shotgun I am holding, not a fucking prayer book!'

'They had me skivvy and serve and grovel. All of them growing rich on the murder of the father I never knew. My mother kept in ignorance and poverty. She will burn in hell!' Solly shouted at me, his lips frothing with rage. He raised his massive hands over his head. I tightened my finger on the trigger of the shotgun but as he raised his hands his coat swirled open, the wind gusted into it, turning it into a sail and forcing him to take a step back. He tried to steady himself but he was at the cliff's edge.

His face looked startled as he comprehended what was happening.

He panicked but had to keep his arms spread to balance himself. The wind ballooned his coat once more and his foot slipped on the loose soil, the ground gave way beneath him and he went backwards over the edge.

'Burn in hell!' he shouted again, his words whipped away by the howling gale and cut short as his body hit the stony beach, eighty feet below.

I breathed out slowly and eased my finger from the trigger of the shotgun. I laid it on the ground and ran over to Kate.

I untied the scarf round her mouth first and like me she took a moment or two to gulp in some air.

'Don't worry, Kate,' I said with a feeble attempt at a smile. 'You won't burn in hell.'

'It wasn't me he was talking about, Jack,' she said finally when she was able to speak. 'He took Susan Dean, too.'

Sergeant Coker got to his feet and looked out over the cliff's edge.

'You better let me take that pistol, Jack,' he said. 'I presume it's not registered to you?'

'No. It's not.'

'I saw the fight. I have the bruises to prove it. How you managed to wrest that gun from him I'll never know. But it was just as well you did, Jack. It was very brave of you – he might have killed us both.'

I nodded. Getting his gist. 'Thanks, Harry.'

'Let's get his prints on the gun and call it in. Then we can go someplace where they have an open fire and a large selection of whiskies.'

66

I was in bed and it wasn't a small brandy and soda on my bedside cabinet. It was a large single malt. No ice. No soda. No spittle.

The tide had been coming in when we had reached the beach and wrapped Solly's huge and lifeless hand around the gun. And the sea was encroaching fast by the time we had called the incident in.

We were clear of the beach and up on the promenade when the army of blues and twos arrived. But the tide had beaten them to it and Solly had been dragged from his resting place by the long cold fingers of the restless sea god.

Detective Inspector Walsh had taken our statements one by one and, by the time we were clear, The Lobster and all the other pubs in the town were locked tight for the night. Sergeant Coker had stayed back to help in the search for Superintendent Susan Dean but I had taken Kate home for a long hot shower and, for myself, a glass of the water of life.

I took another sip of it, felt the warming ease of it as I swallowed. My throat had just about recovered and this was the very best of malts. As smooth as silk.

Kate came in from the shower room, slipped out of her dressing gown and snuggled up beside me. She was pretty smooth herself. The heat from her naked body was like medicine. Like light.

'Do you think they will find her?' she asked.

'I don't know, darling – sounded to me like he had already killed her.'

'Poor woman. OK, you can tell me all of it now.'

I had given a full report in my statement. But Kate hadn't wanted to talk about it until she had got home, had a long hot shower and large glass of chilled wine. I didn't blame her.

When I had finished telling her Solly's story, Kate took a sip of her wine and let out a big sigh.

'Cheated out of his inheritance, cheated out of knowing his father, not knowing who his mother was all these years. I guess he had a right to be angry.'

'I think this went a bit beyond angry.'

'And all because his mother couldn't read.'

'Not uncommon in 1941, if you were from a poor family. Ruth was put out to work at a young age. Meets a teacher at the place where she worked as a cleaner. They fell in love. Star-crossed lovers, as the bald man put it.'

'What was the deal with the U-boats? I heard you saying something about them to Harry.'

'On Beeston Bump they had a Y-station. One of a series of listening posts along the coast here. They intercepted enemy signals which they sent to Bletchley Park. By taking three readings from different posts they could also triangulate the position of enemy craft in the North Sea.'

'Go on.'

'A group of friends – all public-school chums – had formed a business syndicate. They were all important in some way or other in the community. A banker, council members, et cetera. Well, in 1941 it really looked as if Britain was going to lose the war. The country was going to be invaded and the most likely place was on the coast here. The least defendable coastline in the United Kingdom.'

'I know. I was born here, remember.'

'I do. You're a Shannock. I know all about that now.'

'I guess you do.'

'So they are businessmen. Upper middle-class in the main. The world belongs to them. They are used to having their own way and having it with jam on, and champagne to wash it down with.'

'And . . .'

'And Herr Hitler was getting in the way. You have to remember that a lot of upper-class English people didn't want to go to war with Germany in the first place. They had connections with Germany. Business connections, family connections.'

'OK.'

'Preston had family connections. A cousin high up in the German Navy. They were certain England was going to lose the war – a lot of people thought it likely. It was the nation's darkest hour. So the group decided that, if the inevitable was going to happen, why not embrace it. They had a plan to cut the power supply to the listening station on Beeston Bump and get a message to a U-boat to be passed on to Preston's cousin. In short, they were proposing to open the door, as it were, to let the Germans in and have a bloodless beach head established at Weybourne.'

'And in return?'

'Keep their land and money and so forth. Exactly as some of the French had done under the Vichy government.'

'So what changed David Webb's mind?'

'He fell in love. She was just shy of sixteen so he couldn't let anyone know that they were having a sexual relationship. He asked her to marry him.'

'So he fell in love and grew a conscience?'

'Kind of. There was something about Ruth that he only found out later.'

'Which was?'

'She was partly Jewish. Catholic father but a Jewish mother. And that was enough for the Nazis back then.'

'So he tried to stop the plan.'

'Tried to. Got killed for it and was buried in the cave.'

'The other one in the lifeboat got paid off to keep him quiet.'

'And no one was the wiser. Till the cliff fell down.'

'And had David Webb sold his shares, do you think?'

'Unlikely. Signature probably forged.'

'No way of proving it.'

'Not now.'

'Poor Ruth.'

'Poor David.'

'Poor everybody.'

'But they never went ahead with their plan? Or tried to?'

'No. A few days after David Webb was killed, the Japanese air force bombed the United States fleet at Pearl Harbor. The Americans declared war on Japan, became open in their support for the British forces and three days later declared war on Germany themselves. And everything changed.'

'So it was all for nothing. A matter of a few days.'

'Life is like that sometimes, darling. Ruth had gone to her priest and confessed and she had been taken away to have her baby in secrecy. She didn't come back until many years later when she told people that Solly was a nephew and his parents had been killed in the Blitz. It wasn't an unusual story and people had no reason not to believe her.'

'Just a few days,' she said again.

I leaned over and kissed her and wrapped my arms around her. 'I'll sell the Saab,' I said.

67

The next day and the sun was vivid in a lightly flecked sky once more.

Pale blues and salmon pinks and thin wisps of cotton-wool clouds. The wind was fresh but mild, barely making the fallen leaves dance. The air was clean and vital.

The media circus was still in town. Neither Susan Dean's body nor that of Robert Carter had been found. The sea had claimed Solly Green and had not, as yet, seen fit to return him.

Extra personnel had been drafted in from all over East Anglia and the entire area was being searched. But North Norfolk is a land of sprawling countryside. Of woods and farmland, of lakes and hills and spinneys. Huge tracts of uncultivated land. If Solly Green hadn't wanted the bodies to be found, then they could search for a year with little hope of success.

Technically, I was off the case now anyway. Given my involvement in the death of Solly Green, Detective Inspector Walsh had deemed it best that I should cease to be on retainer as a consultant to the police in the matter. I should have gone into the office and got back to my usual routine, but I hadn't. I had spent the morning on the beach and in the woods, as much to think as to help in the search. An unpaid civilian just doing his civic duty.

At lunchtime I dropped into the lounge bar of The Lobster, which was still being kept closed to all but the police and selected locals. A press-free zone. Laura was there talking to a young man of about twenty-eight who I recognised. He was handing her a twenty-pound note. She gave it back to him.

'I don't need it,' she said. 'Just keep your nose clean.'

The young man nodded gratefully and headed off to the garden exit.

I smiled innocently at Laura and gestured to the barman for a pint as I slid onto the stool next to hers.

'New love interest?' I asked her.

Laura pulled a face as if she had just sucked on a rancid grapefruit. 'With Vinny? No, thanks. I was at school with his younger brother, is all.'

Her hair today was still dark purple, except she had put a flash of white through it.

'I know who he is, Laura,' I said.

'Yeah.' She nodded unconvincingly as if just realising it. 'Of course you do. So you solved the case then, big man,' she said, giving me a punch on the shoulder, clearly wishing to change the subject.

'In a manner of speaking. But yes, I do know Vinny,' I said, not letting myself be deflected. 'He does the odd little maintenance jobs up at the caravan park.'

'Do you think Solly Green killed the superintendent?'

'I don't know. I sincerely hope not, but it sounded very much like it to me.'

'Maybe the bodies will turn up seventy-three years later and it will start all over again.'

'What I do think, though,' I said, still not letting myself be sidetracked, 'is that out of season the odd little maintenance jobs dry up for Vinny. What with the caravans all locked up and the park closed for the winter and all.'

'I suppose they must do.' Laura shrugged and took a sip of her drink. I picked up my Guinness and drank a good three inches of it.

'And I also note that, after I put you on the case, the petty vandalism at the caravan park stopped. No graffiti, no smashed windows, no forced locks or broken picket fences.'

'See, what I think it is, is that people got wind I was on the case. And they didn't want to mess with me. I've got a reputation hereabouts, Stretch. You don't mess with Gomez.'

'And what I also think is that you found out what was going on and got him to stop and didn't tell me about it.'

'There can probably be a hundred alternative theories, boss. The main thing is that the objective was achieved. And the client is happy.'

'Is that right?'

Laura shrugged 'Hey. Justice isn't black and white.'

She had me on that. I held my glass up and chinked it against hers.

'I'll drink to that.'

'You coming up Cookie's field later?'

'What for?'

'It's November the fifth. Big bonfire. Hog roast. Music. Dancing. Torchlight procession up the Bump to light the beacon bonfire. Keep the Irish and the Vikings away.'

'The Irish never came here.'

She looked at me pointedly. 'I beg to differ.'

'Only the friendly Irish.'

She punched me on the shoulder again. I would have to do something about that.

'Anyway, I am hardly likely to want to celebrate the torture and murder of a Catholic martyr.'

'He was trying to blow up the Houses of Parliament.'

'And your point is?'

'My point is that Siobhan would love it, and you should stop being such a grump.'

She punched me on the shoulder again.

68

The night sky was frosted with stars.

The moon hadn't risen yet and there was only the faintest of breezes now. It seemed as if giving Solly to the ocean had appeased the angry sea god. For a time, at least. Ancient gods don't sleep for long, though. They soon grow hungry and thirsty again.

A babysitter had been drafted in, one of the younger health visitors that Kate had met through work, and Kate, Siobhan and I were walking along the narrow footpath in the distance past the ancient ruin of Beeston Priory. Another testament to the serial killer King Henry's greed.

In the moonlight its jagged, broken walls and remaining windows took on a sinister presence more suited to Halloween than to Guy Fawkes Night.

Siobhan had gripped my hand tightly as we had walked past the ruin and still held it firmly as we walked down the pathway that was lined with tall hedges and trees on both sides.

Siobhan was holding a torch and she swung its bright beam back and forth as we walked over the wet ground. I was wearing steel-capped leather boots but the girls had Hunter wellingtons in blue and pink respectively. Kate had tried to buy me a pair in green but I had drawn the line at that. I may have agreed to sell the Saab, but there was no way on God's green Earth that I was going to join the flat-cap-and-wellies brigade.

It seemed odd to be going out and celebrating, given all that had happened. But Kate had insisted. Saying it would be good for Siobhan to get back into her normal routine as quickly as possible. She had heard some of what had happened, but I was being cast as the hero of the hour and she was happy with that. I hadn't been a hero at all, of course: I'd stumbled my way to the truth like a blind man crashing through the hedges in a maze.

But Kate was right. Susan Dean's body had not been found. Might never be found, nor that of Carter the dentist. But a line had been drawn under everything with the death of William Solomon Green. Both Harry Coker and I had both determined on the beach that the fall had killed him, and he had missed the night for coming back from the dead by five days.

There were other torches throwing dancing beams in the darkness and the sound of happy children laughing and joking, excited about the entertainment ahead.

There had been some talk of cancelling the event but the town had resisted it. Sheringham has a strong, closely knit community: they had been visited by a terrible sequence of evil events but they had weathered that storm, just as they had withstood the Nazi threat all those years ago, and now they were coming together as a community to celebrate their survival.

At the end of the footpath we came onto the coast road, and had to cross it and recross it to Cookie's field where the main celebrations were taking place.

The field was abuzz with happy chatter, and all eyes turned to us for a moment or two as we appeared. The conversations were whispered but there was no mystery about the subject of them. I headed towards the hog roast and joined the queue, leaving Kate with Siobhan to chat with some friends that she had met at Elaine's hen night. That seemed a lifetime away now, but in fact was just a week or so ago.

As I stood in the line I smiled disarmingly at those who threw me curious glances and after a while they stopped. Which was fine with me. Despite what Susan Dean had accused me of being – I was no showboater.

As I got to the front of the queue and placed my order Harry Coker came up to me.

'Make that four, Jack.'

I nodded at the serving lady who set about filling the bap rolls with sweet and succulent pork.

'Least I owe you, Harry.'

'No, it's not. You found the guy, Jack. You stopped the madness.'

'Still no word on the super?' I asked

'No. Wherever she is, he took that secret with him to the grave. Albeit a watery one,' he added.

We walked over to join the girls and handed round the hog roast baps. I took a bite. Norfolk in a bun.

Harry Coker had eaten half of his before I had swallowed my first bite. He nodded at the smaller beacon bonfire, as yet unlit, that was standing out in clear silhouette on top of Beeston Bump.

'Solly Green may have been a mad, murdering miserable wretch of a human being. But he knew how to build a bonfire.'

Siobhan looked up and asked me jokingly, 'Are they going to burn the Carnival Queen again?' she asked.

I laughed. 'No, darling, they don't do that any more,' I said. 'They banned that back in the 1970s.'

I looked up at the skyline again, at the snaking column of torch-bearers who were wending their way up the hill to light the beacon bonfire.

'Burn in hell,' Solly had said. 'Burn in hell.'

'Shit!' I said, throwing my half-eaten hog roast to the ground and sprinting towards the hill.

Once again I was glad that I had started doing morning runs. Once again I could feel my lungs pumping more oxygen into my bloodstream. Once again I could feel the heat in my thighs and the burning pain as I pushed myself harder to beat the procession of torch-bearers before they reached the bonfire.

I lost.

I charged up over the crest of the hill but the torches had already been set. The flames flickering and growing higher, stirred into crackling life by the breeze that had stiffened. Dancing towards the guy that been propped up in the middle of the bonfire.

I didn't stop, just charged straight through the

flames, grabbed the guy and kicked my way through the piled wood to the other side of the blaze.

The horrified spectators stared at me as if I was mad.

But the weight of the figure told me that it was no stuffed dummy. I laid it gently on the ground and then removed the grotesque mask on the front of its head. Someone in the crowd screamed, shattering the shocked silence.

It was the body of Susan Dean. Her eyes were closed and her face was the colour of milk-white marble.

69

It's not just the smell, it's the light in hospitals that I hate. It is a cold, unnatural and artificial light. There seems to be nothing of healing in it.

I was standing with Kate, holding her hand. Beside us stood Helen Middleton. Looking down at the still form of Ruth Bryson, Helen's long-dead brother's fiancée. It had been seventy-three years since Ruth had seen the man she would have married. Maybe she was seeing him now.

The line on the monitor showed flat. The doctors and the nurses had fussed with various pieces of machinery and had silenced it. The silence hanging in the room now felt like a physical thing. They had removed the drips and oxygen tubes and had left Helen a few moments to say her goodbyes to the woman who should have been her sister-in-law.

She turned to us with tears in her eyes.

'She used to work for us once, you know.'

'You and your husband?'

'No. Long before that. For my parents. When I was about sixteen or seventeen. She used to bring Solly with her sometimes to the house while she was cleaning.'

'A long time ago.'

'A lifetime ago, inspector. Would have been in the late 1940s, early 1950s maybe. Not sure exactly when. But she needed the money. Times were hard back then. That was proper austerity. Rationing still in place. People suffered badly. Not us, of course. We had money. Mother fired her.'

'Why?' asked Kate.

Helen Middleton laughed, but it was a bitter sound. 'For nothing, really. She broke a plate, part of a dinner service. Spoiled the set. And so she was flung out on her ear. She was only a poor young woman, had a child to care for and couldn't even read and write. I didn't even think anything of it at the time. I was too busy with school, and thinking about university and my social life.'

'You were a young woman too, Helen,' Kate said kindly. 'None of this is any of your fault.'

'I just wished she'd have come to us. If we had known about her son . . . but how could we?'

'I know.'

'Can you give me a few minutes on my own, please?'

We walked away, leaving her to sit beside her dead brother's love. Taking her dead hand and holding it without saying a word.

'Why didn't she let people know?' Kate asked me.

I shrugged. I had got quite good at that during my years in the job. 'She was under age, a Catholic, and she was probably worried that they would take the baby away. That the love of her life would be branded a monster. She went away and came back and got on with her life as best she could.'

'All those lies festering all these years.'

'They came out eventually, Kate. I guess the evil was lanced eventually.'

We stopped at the top of the ward by the nurses' station and looked back at Helen Middleton.

Kate gripped my hand harder. 'Secrets can destroy people,' she said.

'As easily as a shotgun,' I agreed.

70

It was some months later.

It was technically spring but someone had forgotten to tell the weather gods. There was a thick hoar frost on the ground and tiny frozen particles in the air.

I was dressed in a traditional suit but I had refused to wear grey. I wanted to wear green as part of my cultural heritage but the proposal was met with as hostile a reaction as Hitler's invasion of Poland had been in 1939. We had struck a balance and we had opted for black. 1930s style to match Kate's wedding dress.

The landlord of The Lobster smiled genially at me as I came in and sat at my usual corner stool.

He put a large glass of whiskey in front of me. 'I've not been idle,' he said. 'The function room's all ready. Bunting, buffet – and chilled Bolly good to go.'

'Cheers,' I said, raising the glass.

'Get it down you,' he said. 'Last drink for the condemned man. On the house!'

I took a small sip. 'Get me a pint to go with it, would you?' I asked. The days when I could knock back multiple half-tumblers of whiskey were a long way behind me. And I had a wedding to go to, after all.

The door opened and she walked in. Killer legs, a cream-coloured skirt and matching jacket. Bright red lipstick, hair that was straight off the cover of *Vogue* magazine. High-heeled, cream-coloured shoes. Eyes that a man could probably dive into.

'Hello, Susan,' I said.

'That's "superintendent" to you, Delaney,' she said as she sat elegantly on the stool next to mine. But she said it with a smile this time.

'Champagne, landlord,' she said.

'We've got some cava somewhere,' he said apologetically.

'Get a bottle of Bollinger from the reception room,' I said.

'Excellent.' He beamed once more and hurried away.

Susan Dean was certainly looking better than the last time I had seen her. Severe head trauma had put her into a coma. Or to put it more prosaically, Solly had hit her savagely on the back of her head with something very hard. He had thought he had killed her and very nearly did. Kate had arrived on the Bump a little while after me. It's hard to run fast uphill wearing wellingtons, after all. She had detected a faint pulse. An air ambulance was called in and Susan was flown to the A&E at the Norfolk and Norwich Hospital. Her skull hadn't been fractured. Luckily she had come out of the coma and was as good as new. Apart from the nights when she woke up screaming, that was.

Screaming at the memory of what had happened, and the imagining of what would have happened had I not pulled her out of the bonfire.

Strangely enough, my own recurring nightmare had not returned since the incident. Perhaps not so strangely, Superintendent Susan Dean's attitude toward me had brightened enormously.

She had finished her first glass of champagne and was sipping on a second when she fixed me with a look. I could see that she had been flirting around the issue of something or other, getting ready to articulate it. Something was on her mind and she was about to let me know what it was.

'I want to offer you a job, Jack,' she said.

I looked at her, a little surprised. 'Really?'

'Really.'

'A consultant on some case? Has something happened that I don't know about?'

The body of the missing dentist had never been recovered although Solly Green's body had washed up on the shore a few days after his death. Spat back by the vengeful god who found the man too unpalatable even for him.

'A proper job.'

'Go on?'

'Your little holiday is coming to an end soon.'

I knew that right enough. I had had Diane Campbell on the phone plaguing me practically every day asking for my decision. And in truth I didn't know what that decision was going to be. Recent events had given me a taste – more a hunger, really – for proper police work again, but I knew how much it meant to Kate and Siobhan to stay up here. Kate's cousin's prospective buyer had fallen through and Kate was pushing me to make a decision.

'I know you are thinking of going back to London,' Susan Dean continued. 'But I want you to stay here. The murders here shook up more than our little town, Jack. Norwich and Yarmouth have been in consultation with us and the county, and we agree that we need some form of CID presence locally.'

'I see.'

'Local knowledge. You can't import that. You know that.'

'I'm not a local.'

'Yes, you are. Especially now. You'll never be a Shannock, Jack. But a large percentage of the people here aren't either. The town is growing. The tourist season is lasting longer and longer. We have the Viking festival, the Crab and Lobster Festivals, the Forties Weekend, the Raft Race, the Christmas events, the Carnival, other things planned. More and more people are coming into the town and we as a police force have to acknowledge that and address it.'

'So where do I come in?'

'Like I say, regional funding has authorised the establishment of a CID unit here. A small unit – nothing like the size of White City or Paddington Green, obviously. But a unit here so that if there is a major incident we don't have to draft in teams from Wymondham ten miles south of Norwich or from Great Yarmouth! We will already have eyes and ears on the ground here. Trained ears. Experienced eyes. But not private.'

'Makes sense.'

'And I want you to head up the unit, Jack. You can select your own team. Be part of the whole process from the ground up. What do you say?'

What could I say?

So I said it best, as the song suggests, for the moment at least, by saying nothing at all.

I was standing at the front pew on the right-hand side of the aisle of All Saints Church in Beeston Regis.

I flicked away the small flecks of snow that had settled on my shoulder as I had made my way from my car to the church. The car was a Volvo, almost new, traded in for my old Saab, and had been driven by my best man.

Sergeant Harry Coker was standing beside me, looking uncomfortable in a suit that matched my own. I had considered asking my cousin to be best man but had decided against it. We had opted for a small ceremony and so no members of either Kate's or my family were there. The church was filled with people, though. Most of them friends of Kate, who had taken to small-town and village life like a mallard making a nest.

I looked behind me. Susan Dean was sitting in one pew, smiling at me but giving me the look. She wanted an answer. Sitting next to her was Diane Chambers with her partner, a PC who worked in the records office at White City, and Sally Cartwright, my old DC. Holding baby Jade and looking as youthful and fresh-faced and innocent as ever. I hoped she would always be that way but I knew how much the city of London and our job took its toll. You had to grow a hard carapace and sooner rather than later.

Amy Leigh was in the pew behind me. She gave me a thumbs-up and winked. Then the music started. Mendelssohn's Wedding March.

Kate had chosen it, of course. Along with the flowers, the hymns, the wedding-breakfast menu. She had asked for my input. Demanded it. But when push came to shove she was far too much of a control freak to allow me to make any decisions that she hadn't already suggested.

I didn't mind. Seeing her happy, seeing that happiness reflected in my daughter Siobhan's eyes and in the happy smiles of our baby brought a warmth to my body that no drug could replicate.

I looked back and smiled as she came in. She was wearing a pearly gold art-deco dress. Her long curly hair framed her radiant face with a floral headband. She looked like she had stepped out of a 1930s film. Olivia de Havilland in *The Adventures of Robin Hood*, only brunette.

She walked slowly up the aisle. Behind her Siobhan in matching bridesmaid dress walked, carrying a wedding posy. Laura Gomez was Kate's other bridesmaid, dressed completely in black – but she had dyed her hair pure white for the occasion. Hugh, Kate's partner at the surgery, was standing in as father of the bride to give her away.

She came up and stood beside me and I couldn't stop smiling. Her beauty took my breath away.

The vicar coughed politely and finally I turned towards him.

'We are gathered today with family and friends to witness the exchange of the marriage vows between Kate Walker and John Delaney.'

I hardly took in what he was saying, watching his lips moving but hardly hearing a word. But when Kate took my hand and said 'I do,' I understood everything.

I was home.

ACKNOWLEDGEMENTS

Thanks firstly to my lovely editor on this book, Selina Walker, who, over a very pleasant lunch, suggested we winkle Jack Delaney, as it were, out of his comfort zone in crime-riddled London and transplant him to the wild and rugged coast of North Norfolk; and making it such a very satisfying and enjoyable journey too. Thanks also to Beth Kruszynskyj (pronounced Kruszynskyj) for meeting him at the train station and making sure he was settled in, and, as ever, of course a big thanks to all the team at Arrow/Random House!

Also, as ever, a very big thanks to Robert Caskie and team PFD. To my long-suffering partner and her mother, who – in the absence of an almond croissant – provides a very acceptable Eccles cake or two. To Irish John for his comprehensive research and knowledge of the local hostelries.

And a very big thank you to the town and community of Sheringham. Very much 'Little Britain' with a big heart!

A crime book needs a villain or two but the bad guys in this one are entirely fictional. As mentioned in the book the stretch of coast here is truly the least defendable area of the entire coastline of the British Isles but – even in the darkest hours of the Second World War – not only the famous, and vital, Y stations but the men and women of the region stood shoulder to shoulder against the very real threat coming across the narrow stretch of the North Sea from mainland Europe.

Thousands of people, nowadays, invade Sheringham throughout the year – on high days and holidays on the various festivals and in the 'Season' to enjoy this magnificent part of the country. But it is a most welcome and friendly invasion. No small wonder then, that even when the town is quiet during the dark days of winter Jack Delaney can sit in front of a roaring fire in his local inn, enjoy the banter of the regulars, and feel, as so many do, at home!

Mark Pearson
March 2014